Evil in a
Small Town

Stormy Raines

www.stormyraines.com

Table of Contents

I know I have a few people to thank, for helping me with this book. I will have many more books and thank you pages to thank everyone.

This thank you page is going to Faye Tigert. All the little notes and letters you sent me help to push me on, so thank you Faye Tigert.

Chapter 1

∞

Finally, this day is over, or that is what I think to myself as I fall into the driver's seat of my sixty-nine Z28 Camaro. I close my eyes and take a deep cleansing breath as I talk to myself out loud, "You know, sometimes owning your own business in the town that you grew up in is monotonous, but today was not that day." I shuffle my body around in the seat and lay my head down on the steering wheel as I start my car. Then I smile to myself as it roars to life. I love the sound of this car. It relaxes me. Hurriedly, I back out of the parking spot where I have parked forever and I enjoy the music and the ride home.

I own a little shop in downtown Hollow Springs, Texas. It started out years ago as a cute kitchen boutique; you know the kind that carries all the new gadgets and *the latest kitchen tools. It was a fun little store then. Now my cute little boutique has morphed into a house and kitchenware monster. I carry everything that you would need to redecorate the inside of your home and the home of the likes of Bunny Trapper.*

I am redecorating the inside of her newly remodeled forty eight hundred square foot home. She is a wonderful little old woman in her mid-eighties, mind sharper than yours or mine. She has the southern woman died blue hair that is thinning on the top so she poofs it higher than it should be. Apparently, that makes it appear like there is more there. Bunny Trapper stands five foot nothing, and she knows just what she wants and I had better be able to find it. Believe me when I tell you, you find a way to get whatever she wants. She owns the First United Bank of Hollow Springs. Her son manages it now, but do not think for a second that he makes a move without her knowledge.

Today Miss Bunny and I were on the hunt for a rock wall waterfall for her entryway. Why she would want a rock wall waterfall is beyond me. It could not be just any waterfall either. It had to be eight feet tall, the height of her entryway from floor to ceiling. I have found plenty that are perfect for what I think she is looking for, but it is just not the one. After a twelve hour hunt, I think we finally found it and I could not be happier.

My drive home is just a few minutes, and sometimes that is not long enough. So I pull into my driveway, hit the button attached to my visor to open the garage door, and pull into the garage. I sit in my car for a second as I do some deep breathing exercises.

For some reason I cannot shake the feeling of weight on my shoulders. A burning in my chest floods over me. My nerves feel like they are close to the surface of my skin. In addition, my chest feels *heavy as if I need to keep breathing deep to push the elephant off me.*

I finally decide to step out of my sixty-nine Z28 Camaro, jet-black with two white stripes down the middle. I gently run my hand across the hood because this car is my baby. The only thing I have ever done to this car other than regular maintenance is have air conditioning put in when I was in high school. Of course, living in Texas, air conditioning is one thing you need. When it is one hundred and five degrees in the shade, I am thankful for that upgrade. This car was my dad's and the only thing I have left of his. When my sister and I lost our parents I made sure, nothing happened to this car. I hate to say this is the only car I have owned, but it makes me feel close to my dad when I drive it.

I close the garage door and climb the two steps into the house. The house that I share with my sister, the only family I have left. She and I are alike in ways. We share the same first letter in our *names, mine is Sarah, and hers is Samantha. We attend church together on Sunday mornings. Both of us get our haircut at the same beauty salon, although we may share that because we live in the same small town and there is only one beauty salon around. In addition, to that we both own our own businesses. This is where our likeness changes. Her business is not something I approve of. Nevertheless, she knows that and* respects me enough not to really talk about her work.

I think she is the best looking of the two of us. She has light green eyes and the prettiest natural auburn hair that flows down the middle of her back, and an olive complexion that comes from the Irish side of our family. My features blend into each other. Even though we are only minutes apart, we do not look alike. Sometimes I secretly wished we did. We do share the same hair color but I have brown or hazel eyes. To me they look a little *dull at times. I have more of a pasty skin color than olive, she is an inch shorter than I am, and her body is much more curvaceous than mine is. I am more of a tall, no figure girl, but hey, that is just me. I am getting to where I like me.*

When I walk into the kitchen from the garage, I can feel the pain in my chest worsen, I try to take a deep breath but to no avail. I look around for Samantha then I yell for her, "Samantha! Samantha!" She does not answer which is not like her. Most of the time, Sam is in the living room watching television. Sometimes she is in the kitchen cooking. I look behind my back into the garage. Her little BMW Z4 is in her parking spot. Unlike me, Sam changes cars as if she changes underwear. This is her newest investment and I really think it is ugly and little, but she likes it and I guess that is all that matters.

The pain in my chest deepens. I franticly start crying out "Samantha, Samantha where are you?" as I start to walk into the kitchen. Suddenly, I hear a faint gurgling sound coming from the other side of the house. It sounds like it is coming from down the hallway. The sound panics me. I run through the kitchen into the living room screaming at the top of my lungs now holding my chest trying to keep my heart from pounding out. "SAMANTHA! Where are you?" The faint sound is getting closer as I run through the living room into the hallway. I can still hear the sound but I do not see Sam.

I run toward her bedroom thinking that has to be where she is.

Is Sam ok? I say to me, "Please Lord let her be ok. She is all I have." As I reach Sam's bedroom door I can see it stands slightly cracked open. The sound I hear is coming from her room. I close my eyes as I pray to myself. Then I reach for her doorknob to her bedroom and I push the door open. I am still clinching my chest with one of my hands. My heart falls as I collapse to my knees. What I see in front of me is much worse than what I could have ever imagined.

I place my hand on the doorknob while I look around the room. Sam has a king size bed in the middle of the room with a four-poster bed frame. She has an elegant high boy in front of her bed in a deep dark walnut; there is blood splattered across the front of it. There is also blood running down the mirror of the dresser. On the far side of the bedroom are two ceiling to floor windows, they are open. I can see the sheer curtains flowing deep into the bedroom almost touching the bedspread. They also have blood splashed on them. There is blood everywhere I can see.

I am still on my knees when my arms drop to my side. Tears wail in my eyes. Right in front of me lays my only sister covered in blood, and we are not talking about a little blood either. She is wearing what looks like a white t-shirt, but I really cannot tell. It is soaked in red plasma. The face that was once so beautiful to me is now swollen her *eyelids appearing as if they are going to burst at any time. There are lesions around her neck that are bleeding too. I cannot quite tell what they are, but know they are not cuts. Her arms have cuts, and there are cuts through her shirt. It looks like she was whipped. What happened to her? Was she whipped? Who would do this to her?*

She has her blood soaked hand reached out to me gasping for what looks like her last few breaths. My body falls toward her, because I cannot move. The sight of her makes me immobile. I reach out for her hands and grab her blood soaked fingers. I pull myself toward her and draw her broken frail body into me carefully trying hard to keep from hurting her more. She winces in pain as I tilt her head up so she can breathe, or so she can try to breathe. She attempts to look up at me through inflamed eyes and tries to speak as I touch her face gently, "Samantha doesn't try to speak, please."

I reach my hand around her head to get my cell phone out of my pocket. She is still trying to speak. "Ssshhh! Samantha don't talk. We need to get help. I am calling 911," my voice cracks. I am trying to keep from just yelling out for help.

I put the phone to my ear and on the second ring a voice answers, "911 what's your emergency?"

I cannot hold the scream in anymore. I yell into the phone, "PLEASE HELP! MY SISTER is dying!"

The dispatcher stutters as she speaks, "Ok! Ok ma'am, what has happened?" You can tell she is trying to stay calm but she wants to scream for help too. She sounds young and for a second I hate that she has to take this call.

"I don't know. I came home and could not find my sister. I heard a gurgling sound from somewhere in our house and I found her on the floor in her bedroom. She has been..." the words came out in a burst of tears, "beaten. There is blood all over the room." As I look *around the room, I see blood splattered from the doorway to the curtains; and from the looks of Sam, it just might be all her blood.*

The woman on the other end of the phone clears her throat, gains her composure, and says, "Ma'am, I am sending help. They should be there in two minutes. You need to go to the door to let them in when they arrive."

"No. I can't leave Samantha!" I yell into the phone.

"Ma'am, your sister needs you to answer the door. She needs help."

My heart gets an immediate rush of adrenaline as I realize she is right, my sister does need me. I look at Samantha, her head in my lap. I gently stroke her matted hair, "Sam, I am going to let the emergency people in. I am going to move you so I can get up." Her face is solemn, but what I can see of her eyes tells a different story. There is fear in her eyes. She grabs at my shirt with what little strength she has as I pick her head up off my lap. I can see *she does not want me to leave her alone. I stroke her hair one more time before I gently lay her back on the floor. "Sam, I am going to let Charlie in. I am sure he is the one working tonight."*

I hear a sound outside sirens I think. I start to get up and let them in. I do not have to let the paramedics or the police in the house, the front door stands cracked open. I guess whoever was here with Sam left through the front door.

That was brave. The front door faces the street.

The paramedic for Hollow Springs is Charlie Rhodes. Sam and I grew up with him. He is a heavier man with dark brown hair. He was a football player in his younger years. I always laughed at that because a little secret about Charlie is that he also wrote poetry in high school. To think he knocked people to the ground as a linebacker, then would write about the wind and butterflies. That was always a little ironic to me.

Charlie has always spoken in a small voice for his size. It can be a little annoying at times; but right now, it is so soothing to me. Charlie is not married, nor has he ever been. I hope one day he finds someone that is worthy of him. He is one of the last good men. I always felt like he had a crush on me only because he would write poems for me. However, he is just not my type.

Charlie, Sam, and I grew up with most of the people in this town. Sometimes that is a good thing, but right now, I am sure this is hard on Charlie seeing Sam like this. Charlie gently kneels on one knee beside me and puts his hand on my shoulder, "Sarah we can take care of Sam. You need to let her go and let us do our jobs."

I am rocking her uncontrollably. My hand is on her neck at her corroded artery so that I can feel her heart beat. I am scared to death that it will stop in the next few minutes. It felt like a lifetime waiting on the ambulance. Her heart has not stopped yet, she is still holding on. I look up at Charlie. "I am not sure I can let her go, Charlie." I burst into tears as I finish speaking, "I can't lose her. She is all I have."

Charlie touches my cheek, "I promise we will do everything we can. Trust me, I don't want to lose her either."

I pull myself up with what little strength I have left. I look around the room that is now full of people and equipment. They are working on Sam in speeds that people should not move. Charlie is talking to Sam telling her everything that he is doing. There is a woman with Charlie running around as he tells her what to do. I really do not know what he is saying, but you can tell he is in his element. The woman comes in with a gurney and I have to move out of the way to let her in.

I feel the room closing in. I can smell the sharp smell of iron and bodies. I watch Charlie gently roll my sister onto her side with all these wires coming out of her from everywhere. Her shirt is missing now, as well as her pants. Sam would die right now if she knew that she was just in her panties and bra.

Sam now has an orange box looking thing around her head. Charlie moves Sam onto her side by her shoulders, he places a board of some type under her motionless body, and then he rolls her onto the board onto her back. The woman pulls the straps connected to the board and places them over my sister. They place her hands gently on her stomach. Charlie gently covers Sam with a sheet so people will not see her in her underwear. He and the women gently lift Sam and the board to the gurney. They lift the gurney up and lay all the machines that are monitoring my sister at her feet. Charlie flips me a quick 'we will take good care of her' look and they quickly roll her out of the room and out of the house.

I am spent. The smell of blood has over taken me and I feel my stomach karate chop my throat. I run to the bathroom down the hallway. I sprint to the toilet and release the pain, the smells, as well as the trauma of this moment into the toilet. I sit there hugging the toilet unaware of how long I have been here when I hear Chief Carson cough. Then I hear him knock on the bathroom door.

Chapter 2

∞

Loy Carson is the Police Chief of little Hollow Springs. As I said, this is a small town so we do not have a detective or really much of a police force, just Chief Carson and his son Lane Carson. Chief Carson is now around 65, and for his age, he is a good-looking man. His hair of course is fully gray now. When I was a child, it was cool black. His eyes are the color of amethyst, now clouded over by what I am thinking would be cataracts. He is very thin, almost too thin, but he has always been that way. His voice is raspy from years of cigarette use. He looks tired and worn out. I think my sisters being attack in his town; will be something that will take a toll on him.

Now Chief Carson's son, Lane, is a different story. Unlike Chief Carson, Lane has a very aggressive personality. Lane is a little older than we are; neither Sam nor I really knew him. He had graduated before we went into high school. However, his reputation preceded him. One of the more famous stories told about good ole Lane was of him getting into a fight with a guy in a bar outside of town. He beat the guy so badly he was hospitalized for days. I drove by the bar days later and the huge glass window was covered with plywood. I always wondered if he threw him through the window or something. I never asked, and shortly after that fight, Lane was shipped off to another state. Everyone said it was for collage I think it was so he would not be prosecuted. When he came back about five years later, he was named Deputy Chief to his dad. I think it is somewhat funny if you ask me, but maybe he is a changed man. I still try to have little to do with him. His eyes look cold to me.

Hollow Springs is your typical sleepy Texas town. We have an older quaint downtown. Antique shops are our bread and butter, one flower shop that handles the town floral needs, a barbershop, and a beauty shop. They are what we would call segregated, but not for the reasons you would think. The men and the women still split when it comes to haircuts. The women go get their hair done at the Honey Bee about once a week. They fill up on all the town gossip during this time. The men in town will never admit it, but they do the same thing at the well-named Barber Shop. In our little town, there is one stoplight, *and after 9 p.m., that one light turns into a blinking yellow light. The cemetery is in the middle of town and is still where everyone is buried, no questions.*

We have an amphitheater where the town gets together once a month in the summer to watch old movies. It is located in a large city park where kids can play while their parents watch the movie. Parents still feel safe, as their children are feet or yards away playing in the park. If a child is ever hurt at the park, not just the mother runs to see what happened, but all the women in town run to help. We grew up with the old saying "it takes a village to raise a child." There are also two restaurants in Hallow Springs, but only one serves breakfast; and on Saturday mornings, most families go for the best biscuits in the world at the Ol Flower Blossom Inn.

The unthinkable has happened here in our little world. The tears well up again and my eyes flood with water. There is a second light knock on the bathroom door and I *hear this raspy voice say, "Sarah. Can I do anything for you?" It is Chief Carson.*

"Not right now, thank you though." What do you say at a time like this?

Last time I was in this position I was five years old. I do not remember much about that day, just that both of my parents died. I really miss them. Right now, their absence is like a crater in my soul. I would love to feel my mom hug me and tell me Sam is going to be all right. All I can do now is remember my mom.

I let go of the toilet, roll my body over to lean on the wall, put my head back, and close my eyes as tight as I can. I say a little prayer to God. "Whatever you do Lord, don't take Sam from me. Please. Through Jesus Christ I pray, Amen." It is brief, but I am feeling a little better now.

I try to pull myself together. I have to get to the hospital. I am splashing cold water on my face when I hear, "Sarah?"

"Yes Chief Carson."

"I really need you to tell me what you saw here tonight. I know this isn't a good time."

"I don't think any time will be a good time to relive what I saw tonight. Come on in. Please, let us get this over with now. I would like to forget this as soon as possible." I also need to get to my sister. Sam needs me now even though I really want to squeeze into a ball in the corner of the closet and stay there until this goes away.

I am a serial closet hider. I have been from the day our parents died. Sam hated when I would hide in the closet. She would do everything in her power to stop me. I would have a break up in high school, or something tragic happen, that would upset me, and I would hide in the closet. Sam would get so frustrated with me. One day she bought a lock for the closet door. She made sure she got home before me, and then she locked the closet so I could not get into it. She told me, "You are not going into your safe house. You need to deal with your problems, not hide from them." I was so mad at her for doing that, but come to think about it I have not been back in the closet. Sam worried about me when we lost Aunt Lela and had locked the closet just in case.

Aunt Lela was our mother's sister. She had no children, other than Sam and me, nor did she ever marry. She passed away about six years ago. Our parents named her as our caretaker if something should *happen to them both. When they both died, she came to live with us. Aunt Lela thought it would be easier on us; she had no ties in Las Vegas where she was living. She dropped everything and came back to her hometown for her sister's kids that she saw two to three times a year. That really did not matter to her. She always said Carman (her sister, my mother) would do the same for her. She would say to us, "Besides girlies, y'all grew on me; and I didn't think you needed to grow up in Las Vegas. For a single woman it is fine and fun. But for a single woman raising two girls, that is not the place to be." We both really loved her for that. Neither of us ever had any desire to go to Las Vegas. We have always loved our small town.*

It drove Sam and me crazy that Aunt Lela would not date. We would try to push her to go on dates when we got older. Because she was a gorgeous woman she would go; and she may have dated them for a while, but she never married. Sam and I would get so mad at her, because sometimes she would date a guy for months. We would say to each other that this guy might be the one. Then he would be gone after months of dating. She would just tell us, "Girls, you two are all I need in life. I have my hands full with y'all and I am happy with just you in my life. Besides, men just complicate things, and goals." She lived by that motto until the end.

Chief Carson came into the bathroom and sat down in the corner of the vanity. "Sarah honey, what happened here?"

I had my knees up to my chest, one hand wrapped around the other arm, and the other hand resting on my forehead. My eyes closed. "Chief, I really don't know what happened here. When I got home, I had an eerie feeling as if something was wrong. To be honest I had that feeling all day. I yelled for Sam when I came into the house because she is always watching television, cooking, or on the computer when I get home and it was weird for her not to greet me." I paused as tears started flowing down my face.

I have my eyes closed again as I get lost in my own head. It may be crazy, but years ago when Sam took my closet away, I found a little voice inside of me. I call her my inner self. I named her Lola. She is sitting on a couch with a huge poster board that reads, "Pull it together, Sarah." I choke the tears back, pull myself together, and start speaking again.

"I heard her gurgling or something; I don't know what it was. Looking back, I think she was trying

to warn me. But there was no warning me for what I was about encounter." I took another deep breath and finished. "When I got to her room, she was as you saw her. She was having hard time breathing. I was so scared to touch her, but I needed to. I wanted to tilt her head back to help her breathe. She tried to talk to me. I told her not to and I called y'all."

Chief Carson looked at me, "Sarah, I am so sorry that you are going through this again." He paused for a second, "Could you understand what she was trying to say to you? Could you make out anything she was saying at all?"

I thought for a minute and in a defeated voice, I answered. "No. I am so sorry."

Chief Carson got up from where he was perched. He came over to me, knelt down beside me, his eyes were sad as he placed his arms around me. "Sarah you did fine. We are going to find who did this to Sam, and when we do, I just may kill them myself." My eyes widened. I wanted to reply but I did not in fear that if I opened my mouth I would tell him he was going to have to beat me to him. We sat in the bathroom for a while in silence. Chief Carson breaks the silence, "You really need to get up off this floor and go to the hospital. I have to find the bastard that did this to Sam." As he got up to walk out he picked me up off the floor. "Do you need a driver to the hospital?"

"No, I think I can do it alone. Thanks though."

Chapter 3

∞

I get to the hospital just after ten o'clock. Our closest hospital is about twenty-five minutes away in a larger town, Mountain Bloom, Texas. I like Mountain Bloom. This town has some great shopping. I like the commercial shops sometimes, but really, my favorite shops are the ones off the beaten path tucked away on the back roads and side streets. Most people come here to do a little fast shopping and get out. I have found some good finds here for customers of mine. There is a dark side to this town for many of the people here and in the surrounding areas. This is where they go to be bad. From what I hear, Mountain Bloom has a hopping nightlife. Maybe they come here to just be someone different.

I park my car in the back parking lot of the hospital. The reason is stupid and something I have done forever and cannot help it. I do not want anyone hitting my car, or even touching my car. You would be surprised how many times I have gone to get in my car and there are handprints on the window from someone looking inside. I hate that. Really, I do.

I grab my phone from the passenger seat, open the door, and step out into the night. I make my way to the emergency entrance of *the hospital and see the beaming red light in front of me. I am still wearing my work clothes and wishing I had thought to change. The red long sleeve jersey material and knee length dress with my cute new light brown knee high boots does not seem to be comfortable attire for the hospital. These boots are cute, but my feet are thinking they are not cute right now. I tell my feet not to give out on me now, and I promise them a good soak the* next time I have a chance to do a pedicure.

I march into the emergency room entrance and head to the first desk I see. "I am looking for Samantha Wilds."

The woman at the desk is on the phone. She puts her finger up at me in the universal "one-minute" motion. I do not like when people make hand gestures at me. I am a person not an animal, and I want you to speak to me. The woman behind the counter is a heavyset woman. Her hair is bleach blonde and the ends of her hair could use some split end treatment. I cannot take anymore listening to her conversation.

I am not a controversial person, but tonight I am at my wits end. I look at the button on the phone and think that would end her conversation. Next, I do the unthinkable. I push it. The women had her back turned; she never even knew I pushed the button. For a moment, she glares at me. I bite my tongue to keep a stone face. Finally, she hangs the receiver up. "Well I guess she dropped me."

I just chuckled to myself as I reply, "I guess she did. Can you please tell me where Samantha Wilds would be?"

The phone rings again. Calmly, I close my eyes. I can see Lola. She is smashing the phone into tiny pieces with a baseball bat. I want to scream, "Tell me where my sister is!"

She says something to the other person on the phone in Spanish. It has been a long time since my last

Spanish class so I really do not know what she said. However, I am sure it was not nice. She puts the phone down and says, "Your sister has been transferred to Surgery Room 1 for emergency surgery. Straight down the hall, through the lobby, and take a right. There will be another desk and they can tell you more."

I tell her thank you as I am walking away. I can hear her say something else to me but I really do not care what it is. I continue to walk without looking back.

I head down the emergency hallway toward the lobby. When I get there, I am suddenly caught off guard. The lobby is vast and beautifully designed. When you step into the lobby, it takes you back in time. For a moment, you forget you are in a hospital. It is a circular room in a building of squares. You look up at the ceiling and all you see is glass. I stare out of the glass ceiling and all I can see is stars. I am reminded of God in this moment.

Without thought, I drop to my knees, my eyes close, and a prayer comes flooding out of my mouth. I do not pray for me, I pray for Sam, I pray that God will keep her safe.

I open my eyes and once again, I am looking back at the stars. This brings me back to the reality of where I am. My eyes glide down one wall of the lobby. Where you see storefronts made to look like an old town from the fifties. There is a sign above one that reads General Store. *This is where I think you can buy daily supplies. There is a sign above another one that says* Carol's Glorious Gifts *where I can see door wreaths for newborn babies in the window. There is a popcorn cart parked next to Carol's Glorious Gifts. On the other side of the room sits chairs in a half moon shape. There is a flat screen television on the wall in front of them. From there stands an all glass entryway. Across from the entrance is a large wood door. That is the surgery waiting area.*

I am walking fast, almost running. I can hear my boots clicking loudly on the beautifully tiled floor. I want to take them off because of the noise, but I am not stopping. I make it across the enormous lobby where there stands the heavy, all wood doors, and I see a small sign on the door, Surgery and Waiting. *I stand there for a second, close my eyes, take a deep breath, and tell my sweaty hands to hit the button on the intercom. I reach up to push the button when* my cell phone begins to ring. It startles me, but I let it ring. I do not even remove it from my pocket. I stand there for what feels like an eternity, but probably more like twenty seconds or so. Nevertheless, in my state of turmoil and inpatients, it was a lifetime. Eventually a voice answers, "Can I help you?"

I take a breath, "My sister is Samantha Wilds. I was told she was in surgery." A buzzer sounds as the door clicks open.

Right now, Lola is watching a scary movie and eating popcorn. I can hear the infamous death scene music in a macabre movie as I push the heavier than I thought door open, then it gently clicks behind me. My phone dings telling me whoever called left a message. I walk to the desk where a cute, cheery young woman sits. She has a bob haircut poofed in the back. It is light brown with red streaks. Her eyes are rather large for her face, but they shine with wonder.

"Are you here for Ms. Wilds?"

I am blank for a second. Not many people call Sam, Miss. "Yes I am," I say in a shaky voice.

The young woman lifts up her hand and points to the waiting area. "This is the waiting area where Dr. Carmichael will come in to talk with you." I turn to head into the waiting room. She smiles and tilts her head to one side, "If there is anything you need, please let me know. I will get it for you." I do not say anything, just nod at her.

I was expecting the waiting area to be dark and drab, but to my surprise, it was light and open. The room is all white with one wall being a huge window looking out onto the front entrance and a flat screen television on another wall. I can see people walking by the window but they never look in. I think it is mirrored glass. On the other hand, they may know what area this is and they do not want to look at the people in here. I look at the table they have set up next to the television. There is a coffee pot that is empty right now, but not for long. Next to the coffee pot is everything to make a pot of coffee except water. There is a light brown basket containing sugar, creamer (the plain and the doctored up kind), and Sweet'N Low. I grab the pot off the cradle and start my hunt for the water to fill this baby to the top. It looks like it is going to be a long night. I will be in need of the strong stuff tonight. Drinking coffee, this late keeps me up all night, and tonight I need it to do just that.

I step out of the door into the dimly lit hallway. There at the desk is the young girl typing away on the computer she sees me and is quickly on her feet. She runs around the desk to meet me. "Here, let me get that for you," she says as she is grabbing the pot out of my hand. "I will bring it in there and make a pot for ya," she smiles. She takes the pot around the desk to a room and is gone just like that.

I turn to head back to the waiting room when I run smack into a man in scrubs. I topple back a step or two as he grabs me by my elbow to keep me from falling. "Ms. Wilds I take it?"

I gain my footing back. "Um, yes," I respond. All I can see is his face. The rest of him is covered in light blue scrubs and what looks like a paper hat. I am sure there is a purpose for that paper hat. I look down at the ground due to embarrassment where I can see he is wearing light blue booties on his feet too. A small smile comes over my face as I think about how he *kind of looks like a clown without the face paints. I hate clowns. They have always scared me a little. I am thinking his attire scares me a little, but in a different way. If I did not know any better I would laugh out loud, but I know by the get up that he must be Dr. Carmichael.*

He looks at me with a tenderhearted smile, "May we go into the waiting room to sit? Please?"

I answer, looking down at my hands that I have squeezed tightly together, "Yes."

We head to the well-lit waiting area. My phone dings again reminding me that I have an unheard voice mail, but I really do not care at this moment. Half of the world could fall into the ocean at this moment and I would not care. You know if you think about it, half of my world is falling into the ocean.

Dr. Carmichael and I face each other. I am trying not to throw up now. "Dr. Carmichael, is my sister *ok?" With my head down, I have my eyes focused on a speck on the tile floor trying hard not to cry because if I start now, I may not stop.*

You can tell he is trying to find the best way to give me the news about my sister. He clears his throat, "Ms. Wilds, your sister, Samantha, has been severely beaten."

I have both of my hands twisted together. I tighten my grip as I shut my eyes. My heart is pounding out of my chest. Dr.

Carmichael grabs both my hands and my eyes pop open as I look at him in shock. It is so unexpected to have a doctor grab your hands. Dr. Carmichael's eyes lock with mine. "Your sister presented with many open wounds. It took many stitches to close them. She has also lost a lot of blood and there is trauma to her head. We will not know the extent of her head trauma until she wakes up. Right now, we have her in a drug-induced coma. We are going to leave her like this for the rest of tonight and slowly start to bring her out tomorrow if she is doing better. The trauma to Sam's head is extensive. This is why we are keeping her in a coma. We have closed all the wounds and are giving her blood now. She will be in a room in ICU within the hour. Things went great. I just want you to know she is not out of the woods yet. And right now all we can do is pray."

I am listening to every word when I realize my hands are hurting me. I am squeezing his hands harder than I should be. I look down at my hands and quickly release my death grip. "I am so sorry." I rub his hands as I apologize.

"That is quite alright, Ms. Wilds. I am used to that. You do have a strong grip though, I will say," he smiles as he replies. He stands to leave the room. I notice the bouncy young woman is now at the table making coffee for me. I did not even realize she had come in the room. He smiles at her and she smiles back, then he is gone around the corner. I look at the television. The *news is on and they are talking about Syria. For a second I watch and my thoughts are on those poor people over there, not here in this tragic life I am living.*

Cute bob cut pulls my attention back to this world, "I feel sorry for those people. It is so sad what is happening to them. And how could anyone treat people like that?"

Our eyes meet at the same time. You can see in that moment, she remembers that this is how my sister was treated. I smirk, "You would be surprised what people will do to others."

She tucks her chin into her chest as she walks out. I probably should not have said that. She did not mean what she said like that, but for some reason my patients are wearing thin.

I reach in my pocket and grab my cell phone to see the time, eleven thirty. Well it is not as late as I thought. I see the little voice mail icon at the top. I slide the screen to unlock it and when it opens to the homepage, I tap the voice mail icon.

I put the phone to my ear, "You have one new voice message. Message one," the computer pauses, then I hear a voice I do not recognize. It is a deep, breathy voice like Sam Elliott whispering in your ear. Not a Marvin Gay singing in your ear kind of voice.

The man is well spoken, "Sarah I will make this quick. I know what happened to Sam. I want you to remember the phone number I am calling from Ok. Do not save it to your phone. I will be calling you back soon. I hope you will trust me enough to answer. Tell no one of this call. I need you to know my men are working on what happened. I hope to talk to you soon."

My mouth is gaped wide open. I bring the phone down to eye level and hit the number one button on the screen to replay the message. Thankfully, there is a chair underneath me to sit in as I am starting to feel a little dizzy. I think I would have fallen on the floor if it had not been for that chair. I then realize I am only dizzy because I am *holding my breath. I inhale a deep breath and close my eyes. The trauma of the last few hours comes to the surface of my skin. I am feeling numb and tingly all at the same time. I begin to rub my arms to get the feeling back in them.*

Lola shows herself again. She is in a kitchen standing in front of a bar area looking back at me with her apron on. She has a butcher knife in one hand, arm bent at the elbow, and the knife blade pointing up towards the ceiling. Her other hand is leaning on the counter and her eyes are as wide open as her mouth. I think we are both in shock. She stabs the knife into the counter as her face-hardens, and I notice I too have a hardened look on my face.

I check my phone again. At the top of the drop down menu, there is a missed call icon. I drag down the menu and the number shows in a little window on the phone. I push on the number and it takes me to my call history. He told me to delete the number form my *phone, but I really want to call it back. I tell myself to be patient; he said he would call me. I probably should tell the police, or I could take care of this on my own.*

Lola is screaming at me. "Oh hell no! You are not calling the police! We are following this lead ourselves!"

I look at the time he called, ten twenty-nine. It is now eleven forty-seven. I think to myself, "He said he would call back soon."

"Well it is soon," I say aloud to my phone. Then I hold my finger down on the number and hit delete. I shake my head, sigh, and put the phone back in my pocket. I throw my head back on the chair willing the man with the sultriest voice I have ever heard to call back. I need him to call back. He knows what has happened to my sister.

Chapter 4

∞

I am standing at the window of the waiting room watching the people outside. It is late now so there are not many people, just a few nurses and hospital staff taking their break. It must be cool outside. Everyone I see is huddled together in a circle trying to keep warm. You can see smoke billowing up from the circle. I do not know why, but I find myself staring at them. However, my thoughts are not on them. I cannot get that phone message out of my head.

I almost jump out of my skin as a voice speaks from the waiting room doorway. "Ms. Wilds, Samantha has been moved to ICU now. It is on the third floor," the young woman tells me.

"Ok, thanks," I reply turning from the window and walking

toward the door to exit back into the lobby.

I open the heavy door that leads out into the hallway. I look around and spot the elevator. I am so ready to see Sam. I just hope she looks better than the last time I saw her.

I can feel my heart pounding in my ears. I am almost running to the elevator and I push the arrow button to go up. I can hear it moving as I impatiently tap my foot waiting for it. The elevator dings and the door open.

"Finally!" Lola groans in my head. I grin to myself. Luckily, for me she only exists in my head.

The ride up to the third floor seems to take forever. The elevator dings again. The door opens to another welcoming waiting room with an oversized door standing passed the waiting room in front of me. This time there is a keypad to one side of the door on the wall. I glance around the waiting room and notice two men wearing suits and *look a little out of place. I look at them and they notice me, but we do not speak. I walk through the waiting room and head for the massive door that stands between my family and me.*

I press the button on the intercom and once again, a voice speaks to me, "Can I help you?"

I speak into the box, "My sister is Sam, and I mean Samantha Wilds. I was told she was moved up to ICU."

"Yes ma'am she is here. It is after hours though. You need to

come back in the morning. First visiting hours begin at six a.m."

I want to scream and pull the box off the wall. Lola has steam coming out of her ears and her head is spinning around like the exorcist. I push her out of my head, press the button one more time, take a deep breath to calm myself, and say as calmly as possible, "She is my sister. In addition, she is all I have. I really need to see her. Please. I need to see that she is alright."

Static comes across the box, and then a voice says, "OK. We will *let you in for five minutes." I am jumping up and down when the door clicks open. The two men in suits do not even look up from the paper they are reading. I open the door and I am plunged into another world. This is the most efficient area I have ever seen. First, the desk area is in the middle of the room sectioned off into a hexagon shape. Every side of the hexagon has a computer screen as well as other machines that are printing something or beeping at you. The* sounds are a little annoying and over whelming. If my sister was not in here, I just might turn around and leave the way I came in.

There are no rooms, just curtains sectioning off what would be rooms. An older lady looks up from one of the machines, "You looking for Samantha?" she asks. I close my mouth and reply, "Yes, Ma'am." She walks around the machines looking at me with concern. Her eyes are noticeable with sweet pale blue irises. She is in her mid-fifties it looks like, with long *sandy blonde hair tied back with a ponytail holder. "Right this way," she smiles.*

We walk around the room to one of the curtained areas. The woman pulls the curtains back and in the bed lies what may be my sister, but I am not sure. She has wires hanging from everywhere. One of her machines looks as if it might be helping Sam breathe because her chest was inhaling and exhaling unnaturally. There are monitors everywhere - monitors for her heart, for her breathing, IV monitors, and nurses at all times too were monitoring her. When you look past all the monitors, the person laying there still did not look like my sister. Her face is much more swollen than before, and her eyes are taped shut. However, even if she wanted to open them, she could not because of all the swelling. You can see more bruising now all across her. Her body is wrapped in bandages from head to toe. I clasp at my chest. I am in pain for her.

I close my eyes and I see Lola. She is on her knees with her hands clasped together, head down, and doing what I would like to be doing – praying.

The nurse notices my pain. She places her hand on my shoulder. "I know she looks different, but that is Samantha. She can hear you if you would like to let her know you are here."

I turned to her with tears in my eyes, "You really think she will know I am here?"

"Sure she will," she responds with a soothing smile.

I walk further into her room. Well, it is not really a room, more like a cubical. I take a deep breath, grab her hand, and just start talking to her. I tell her I love her. I cannot look at her for fear I will start to cry. I tell her to hang on and fight for me, and I really need her. In addition, I let her know I am going to find out who did this to her.

I believe I have visited for more than five minutes, and then a nurse comes in to tell me it is time to leave *so that Sam can get her rest. I kiss her hand and promise her I will be right outside, and if anything happens, I am seconds away. I tell her one last time that I need her to fight as hard as she can because I cannot live without her.*

I walk past the nurse, she smiles, and I smile back. I look back at the cubical where my only family lays, leaving her here without me staying is breaking my soul but I know she is in good hands. Unwillingly, I head out of the ICU and finally exhale as I lean up against the ICU door. I close my eyes for a moment as I gather myself. After about a minute, I walk toward the ladies room. The two men are still sitting in the waiting room with only one reading the paper now. I do not want to sit in the waiting room with them. It is not that I am scared; I just need to be alone right now. I think I am going to go find myself some coffee after I stop by the restroom. Maybe when I get back from getting coffee the two men will be gone.

I stay in the restroom for a while as I wash my hands to warm them up. I put on a little lip-gloss and run my fingers through my hair in hopes of making myself presentable once more. I step out of the restroom and head toward the elevator. As I reach out to push the Down button, one of the suited men suddenly, reach from behind me and pushes it. I whip around to look at him. He is the older man with a bur haircut. They would call this high and tight in the military movies. It is all gray and he is not much taller than I am with a stocky build. He turns to me and smiles sympathetically. His eyes are almost sad and make me wonder what he has been through in his life.

The elevator dings bringing me back to reality, and at the same time my cell phone rings. I franticly reach into my pocket for the phone, but it is stuck in the corner of my pocket. I fumble it out as the man in the suit and I step into the elevator.

I can see Lola in my head running around her living room

jumping up and down screaming, "Get the phone! Crap, you know it is him! Get the phone out of your pocket, Crazy!" She is pulling her hair away from her head as she falls to her knees.

Finally, I get the phone out of my pocket on the third ring and slide the touch screen to accept the call as I scream into the phone, "Hello! Hello! I am here!"

As I step into the elevator, the man in the suit steps in behind me. The doors to the elevator start to close and the suited man pushes the button to the lobby for me. I then hear the voice on the phone.

"Sarah. I am very glad you trust me enough to answer. I must make this short and sweet. The man in the elevator works for me. I need you to go with him. I promised your sister I would keep you safe. His name is Tucker, and he will bring you to me. There is another man that will stay with your sister. His name is Adams. He also works for me. Please trust I will not hurt you. Go with Tucker. If you do not go with him, I am not sure I can keep you safe. I would hate to know I broke a promise I made to Sam."

The phone goes silent just as the doors to the elevator open into the lobby. My instinct is to run, and run fast screaming for help. The man named Tucker is looking kindly at me with those sad eyes that leave me wondering about his past again. I look at him for a second trying to gauge what kind of man he is. I take a deep breath, turn from him, and start to walk out of the elevator.

Tucker puts his hand gently on the small of my back leading me to the massive front exit on the other side of the lobby. We step out of the automatic doors into the cool night air. It is January in Texas. Most of the time, the nights in Januarys are in the high forties to low fifties. Tonight is low forties and I forgot my jacket.

Tucker and I still have not spoken. We have walked half way across the parking lot and I begin to shiver. Tucker finally breaks the ice first by asking, "Do you need my jacket, Ms. Wilds?"

I reply with a simple, "No thank you."

What do you say to someone that may be kidnapping you? I see Tucker removing something out of his pocket. My heart starts to beat faster, and I glance around the parking lot. We are far from anyone now; no one will even know I am gone. I would not be missed until my sister woke up, and who knows when that will be. I let out a sigh of relief when he pulls the keys from his pocket.

He clicks the doors open to a black Mercedes SUV. It is a cool car. I say to him as I point over to my car just a few rows down, "Hey my car is over there. We can take it."

He smiles shyly and says, "Ms. Wilds, I would love to drive your car. It brings memories back for me. However, I am used to this one's handling. Please get in."

He opens the back door and I climb into the back seat. The smell of new leather washes over me. This is the softest leather I have ever sat on.

"Tucker, I can ride in the front."

He laughs, "No ma'am. You need to ride in the back in case something happens. I can keep you safer back here."

I sit down and sink into the leather seats as they cocoon around me. I want to fall asleep, but with Tucker's comment and the recent phone call, I could not if I tried.

The car gently roars to life and Tucker smoothly starts the decent away from the hospital. I am overcome with fear. Without thinking, I look back at the hospital. This could be my last minutes, my last hours, what was I thinking getting in this car? I must be glutton for punishment. I have made my bed. I take a deep breath and lay my head back on the cocooning leather seats. Now I have to lie in that bed.

With my eyes closed, I can see Lola in her gee standing inside a

Shoji with one hand reaching toward the sky and the other pushed out in front of her. She has her leg bent and bringing it towards her chest. Sometimes I wish she were not locked in my head. She just might whip this guy's ass. I am not the ass whipping kind. Although, I may try my hand at it if I find out who has done this to Sam. I think to myself I may get a chance to try my hand at it soon because I could be heading to his house right now.

Fear washes over me, and just out of habit, I reach for the door handle. Of course, it is locked. I do not know what I would have done once I opened it, jumped out of this moving vehicle. Yeah right. I would be lying in a bed next to Sam if that happened, and not finding out what happened to Sam.

Tucker is smart. The child lock must be on because it does not even attempt to open. I take a deep breath and lean my head back on the cocooning leather seats again. I think back to the phone conversation I just had with sultry voice, and something he said stands out to me. He said he made a promise to my sister. When did that happen? I realize in that moment I have many questions like, what is going on here? Since when do my sister and I need to be kept safe, and who is trying to harm us?

Chapter 5

∞

The SUV is charging through the night. Tucker periodically looks in the rear view mirror; I think he can feel me staring at him. I am just trying to figure this man out a little. I am having a hard time figuring him out. He wears a poker face well. Most of the time I am good at judging people, but this man is beyond me. He is a wall. I want to ask him a million questions, but I can see he is not going to answer any questions I have.

We drive in silence for what seems endless. A couple of times I tried to close my eyes, but they would pop right back opened. All I can see is Sam lying on the floor looking so helpless. That is so un-Sam-like. Helpless is not who she is. She is the strong one, the one that keeps me from retreating inside myself. She is fun loving and never met a stranger.

My mind glides back to us as kids. Sam is in our kitchen standing on top of the counter and on the telephone with a boy, I like. Sam is telling him the reasons he should ask me out. I am running around on the floor chasing her around the counter as she is gracefully jumping and running across the counter tops. She is laughing at my discomfort, and enjoying the moment too much.

"Sarah you need to live a little. Put yourself out there."

I giggle to myself. If she could see me now. When she wakes up and I tell her this, she is not going to believe me.

Tucker turns the SUV down a narrow road outside of town. I think to myself that this is it; this is going to be the moment of truth. I look around to find something I could use as a weapon, but there is nothing in the car. I do have my car keys. I pull them out of my pocket and place them between my fingers. If I need them, I think I could use them.

Tucker drives a short distance down the road when the SUV pulls up to a black ornate gate with an intercom and keypad, my favorite. He punches in a code and the gate swings open. There is a small creek as the gate opens and it unnerves me a little. We drive down a dark driveway before the house comes into view. My mouth drops as my eyes focus on the property that is in front of me.

We swing around the circle drive as Tucker pulls up close to the house. The house is all lit up with *two gorgeous trees standing at either side of the house, illuminated by the light. I reach for the door handle to step out of the car. I want to take in the view of the house from outside the car. I pull on the door handle a couple of times, the door does not open. Tucker finally comes around the SUV and lets me out. I can see the detail of the house as the light dances around. My eyes catch a movement to one side. With the ornateness of the house, I never noticed the front door was open.*

There was a man standing in the doorway.

The man begins walking down the stairs making his way toward me. I back up to the door of the SUV. Fear rushes over me and the pounding in my heart begins again. That feeling is becoming so familiar to me tonight. Tucker meets the man at the foot of the stairs. They shake hands and exchange words for a moment. Tucker steps away and starts his decent up the stairs and into the house. The man is still a few steps away from me. I grip *my keys tighter in my hand, waiting for what is coming next.*

My mind is racing all over the place. I look up toward the house as Tucker is walking into the doorway. The man and I are the only two left. I want to run, but I do not think I would get very far.

The figure walking to me looks fit. I begin to think of my sister again and tell myself to be strong; this is for her. I scan what I can see of his body looking for marks of some kind. I learned that from self-

defense class. The pounding of my heart speeds up. He stops in front of me and my hand opens as he stops, keys dropping to the driveway making a clacking sound as they hit the concrete. A weird breeze begins to blow as he stands there in front of me. I can smell the faint hint of flowers and wonder if it is coming from him or the paper whites that are scattered around the property.

His voice does not do him justice. He is a salient man, much more striking than I expected. His hair is cut very short. It looks like it *may be brown, light brown – I cannot really tell in the dark. His eyes are the color of amber. He is wearing a white t-shirt that fits loose on his body, but with the breeze that is blowing, I can see the strong lines of his chest. He is wearing jeans that are free on his hips. His skin is caressed with a touch of honey; Venus herself sculpted his features with sharp strokes.*

I suddenly remember that my keys dropped to the ground. We both bend down to pick up the keys.

Bent over we turn to each other, our eyes meet, and a heat comes over me. We are staring at each other when he hands me my keys. I feel his hand wrap around mine, and when he releases his hand, his fingers move smoothly over mine. I can feel the warmth of his skin. After he releases his hand, I long for his touch for another moment.

We stand and he clears his throat and says, "Well I guess you are Ms. Sarah Wilds?"

"Why yes I am. Um... and who are you?"

He laughs as he puts his head down. I take it he forgot I did not know him. He looks up at me and says, "Ms. Wilds I am so sorry. My name is Gideon Glass. I know your sister, Sam."

He gently grabs my arm, "Please come inside. Let us get you out of this cool air. I have a fire still burning in the fireplace; you can warm your bones there."

I walk with him up the stairs and into the house. As we head into the doorway, I stop him and say,

"Hey look, I am having a hard time with all of this. I really don't want to go inside yet,"

Gideon turns to me, clutches both of my arms in his hands, smiles gently at me, and says, "Ms. Wilds, I am not going to harm you. I am not who hurt Sam, but we will find out who did hurt her and take care of them if we need to. Now please, come inside and get warm. Mrs. Tucker has made you up a room in case you want to lie down. We can figure out the rest tomorrow." He

*opens his arm as he opens the door,
"Please, after you."*

*I take a deep breath and cross
the threshold into the house. Gideon
crosses in front of me as we walk
into the foyer. I look at where he is
going and can see Tucker standing
in a doorway off one side of the
kitchen.*

*Gideon turns to me, but keeps
walking backwards and says, "Ms.
Wilds, please make yourself at home.
There is the fireplace. I will be right
with you." Then he turns back*

toward the room that Tucker is
standing in. He walks through the
door and shuts it behind him.

I stand in the foyer, and look
around the room. I cannot take my
eyes off the massive area. You
cannot really call it a room; it is just
one big floor. The inside of this
plantation home has been
completely remodeled. There are no
walls on the first floor; everything is
so modern looking compared to the
outside of the house. As I am
looking around the house, my eyes
stop at the staircase. It is not

modernized, and is impressive as it slinks up one wall in a backward S shape. With robust spindles guiding the way, my eyes wind around with the staircase. Eventually they land on the second floor balcony. It is a wide-open area overlooking the first floor, and under the balcony is a kitchen that anyone could work in. It has granite counter tops from what I can see only the light over the stove is on. All the appliances are commercial grade, but I cannot locate the refrigerator. It must have

one of those false cabinet looks.
Beside the kitchen is a room that I
am assuming is the office. On the
other side of the first floor is a
ceiling to floor fireplace made of
river stone. On either side of the
fireplace rises two ceiling to floor
glass walls.

I decide to walk over to the
fireplace; it just looks so inviting. As
I stand in front of the fireplace, I am
looking at a light colored leather
sectional calling my name. Maybe I
could try to sleep this day away.

However, I am not sure sleep is in my future.

I close my eyes for a second and see Lola. I laugh, as she is on that light colored leather sectional naked, wrapped in a cashmere blanket, drinking hot chocolate. Looking back at me like, what?

When I open my eyes, I see movement on the other side of the room. Gideon has opened the door to the office and is striding toward me. Without thinking, I shift my body so I am standing a little straighter. He is so lithe when he walks. It is like watching a cheetah stalk its prey. I realize I am staring at him when he looks at me and smiles. I look down in embarrassment and can feel my face flushing.

He walks past the couch toward me and for some reason I get the urge to run. I look around the room. There is nowhere to go. I look up and stare at him for a moment, our eyes meet. I am so embarrassed when he catches me staring at him. I put my head down and stare at the *floor. He stands in front of me for a second looking at me before he speaks.*

"Ms. Wilds, I know I told you we would discuss Sam tonight, but I do not have a lot of information right now."

I jerk my head up to look at him. He keeps talking, "I really think the best thing to do right now is try and get some sleep. Tucker is still working on some things. Maybe he will know more in the morning."

*He lightly touches my
shoulders. I am looking through
him now, but he is still speaking,
"Today has been long for you. I
know you do not want to, but you
need to try to sleep. You need to
keep your strength up for Sam." He
clinches my shoulders again,
"Tucker is following some leads as
we speak. Please let me show you to
your room."*

*I have a blank stare on my face
as he looks at me. You can tell he is
trying to judge my reaction. I turn
my head away from him first and*

chew on my lower lip. I wait to reply to his suggestion in fear that if I do right now, fire will fly out of my mouth and set his pretty face a blaze like a dragon. I decide I have to answer so I take a deep breath, and when I turn to look at him, I can feel the daggers behind my eyes.

Not so calmly, I begin, "What? Really? You want me to just go lie down?"

I cross my arms in front of me as I am just getting started. "My sister is lying in a hospital bed beaten half to death," my heart flutters as I say that. I do not let it faze me and keep ranting, "And you really think I can sleep? I understand you don't know me all that well, but let me just say," I take a step toward him, point my finger at him and the words keep flying, "Sam is my life. So now my only mission is to find out who did this to her."

I am almost in tears as I turn away from him toward the glass wall and finish, "Sleep is nowhere in my future so you can tell me what *you know now! Or I assure you, Mr. Glass, I will find out on my own without you or your team."*

A few minutes pass and neither of us speaks. I am still standing at the glass wall afraid to turn around. I rarely lose my temper, but I would definitely categorize this as a lost temper. This happens to me so little. I do not know what to do right now. I thought about walking out, but then I remember I did not drive, I was driven here to protect me. Protect me from what.

Chapter 6

∞

Mr. Glass breaks the silence in the room as he clears his throat and says, "Well Ms. Wilds I think you have made your point."

I pivot around to look at him. He is no longer standing at the fireplace, but sitting on the sofa. He looks bold with both arms open and propped on the back of the couch. He has one leg crossed over his other knee. If I knew him a little, better I would walk up to him and slapped his leg off his knee.

A blink goes by before I reply, "What do you mean, Mr. Glass?"

"Ms. Wilds, please forgive me." He stands and starts to make his decent toward me. He keeps talking as he walks, "I may have been wrong, but I was just trying to think of you." He stands in front of me now with his head cocked to one side and a look of concern on his face. "I *thought you needed some sleep. You have had a long day and there is nothing we can do for Sam right now." He places his hand gently on my shoulder again, "But I can see Samantha knows you well. She told me you were a pistol."*

I tilt my head to one side. I want to comment but I am at a loss for words.

Gideon puts both his hands at his side and begins again. "I know a little more than I wanted to tell you about what happened to Sam." I straighten my stance as he puts his head down and looks at the ground. He looks a little out of his element standing like that. "Sarah, I know you don't want to hear this, I know you don't like your sisters choice of occupation, she has told me that, or let me rephrase - she told me you do not approve of her choice of business."

I put my hand up to stop him. I close my eyes, and shake my head. "Don't tell me her owning a gentleman's club has something to do with this?"

He raises his head up to look at me. "First I need to tell you that I am her silent partner in one of those clubs."

I shoot daggers with my words as I reply, "That kind of place appeals to you? I guess they do. You are a guy, right?"

Gideon chuckles at me, "Sarah, I hate to tell you this but I am not a partner in the club for the girls, I am a partner for the money only."

The one thing I hate about my sister is her choice of business. Sam can do anything, and her choice is to own a gentleman's club. She not only owns one, she owns two, and they both reside in good old Mountain Bloom. Sam is good at keep me far removed from her work. My mind drifts off again to Sam and I as children.

We are in a pasture running away from each other; Sam saying, "Go hide over there, Sarah." I can see a young boy standing in front of a tree. His arms are propped on the tree with his head is leaned into his arms.

After I find my hiding spot, I hear him say, "Fifty! Ready or not, here I come!"

I am lying in the high grass as flat as I can get. I can still see everything. The young boy quickly finds Sam hidden behind a tree. Instead of running away from him, Sam jumps into his arms and they both fall into the high grass. I cannot see them, but out of habit, I close my eyes.

Surprisingly, I hear a boy's voice say, "Samantha, that is not funny." When I open my eyes, I see the young boy walking back toward the house.

Standing off in the distance I hear Sam say, "Come on, it was just a joke! Come on out, Sarah."

I jump when Gideon starts to speak again, "For the last few months Sam has been having problems with one of her patrons. She has received threats. Now threats are just a part of the business, she gets them all the time."

I turn and stare at him, he caught my look, as he recants, "But *the threats were never scary, but more always someone wanting money or one of her girls. Some of the threats have been from girls that once worked for Sam, but she just blows them off. However, these threats are personal, and some of the threats are even bodily harm."*

Fear and anger flew all over me as I turn to Gideon. "So let me get this straight," I have one hand resting on my chest, feeling like I am trying to hold my heart in with this gesture, but the gesture could be to keep me from hitting him. I tilt my head to one side, close my eyes, and add, "My sister has been getting threats from people. And for the most part, you and she both think that threats are alright until you realize one of these sickos are threatening bodily harm to her? And Gideon, I still do not get your part in all this. You are a silent partner to a woman who owns a strip club. So what? You are a coward who can't own his own whore house, so you decide to hide behind a woman and her whore house?"

At this moment, I am feeling sick. I turn to one side then the other looking for the exit. I want out, and I want out right now! I see the front door and begin to head towards it.

"Sarah, what are you doing?" Gideon exclaims as I reach the threshold of the house.

With a smirk on my face, I reply, "What does it look like I am doing? I am leaving this place." I head down the stairs and past the SUV still parked in the driveway. This time neither he nor Tucker is taking me anywhere.

Gideon yells behind me, "Wait Sarah, please. At least let Tucker take you into town or back to the hospital. Do not try and walk. You have no idea where you are going and he is still out there."

I stop in my tracks. My body goes numb as he says, "He is still out there." I have not thought of that. Sam's attacker is still out there. Moreover, I really do not know *where I am, nor have any idea how to get back to town. Quickly, I turn and head back toward the house.*

"Can you please get Tucker to take me back to the hospital?"

Gideon throws the keys in the air and catches them as he walks down the stairs. He smiles at me and says, "Tucker is busy right now. I would be happy to take you though. Please, get in."

I curl up my nose as I climb into the back seat. I am not riding in the front with him.

Once again, I am in the cocooning back seat. All the information, the drama of the day, and the night flood over me. Tears well up in my eyes, I cannot cry now. I want to cuddle up in this seat and sob, but there is no time. Curling up in a ball on the floor is what the old Sarah would do. In a moment, my life has changed. It has become a war zone. I am on the front line. I close my eyes and let the tears fall, and when I wipe them away the crying is over.

"Your sister called me before she was attacked." I must have fallen asleep for a minute because Gideon's words awaken me.

I reply as I run my hands through my hair, "What do you mean Sam called you?"

"She wanted me to meet her…"

I stopped him in mid-sentence, "Did you get to talk to her?"

"No. She left me a message saying she received another phone call and said it was disturbing. Sam

also said she was pretty sure she knew who the caller was."

I am chewing my fingernails listening, hoping he knew whom the caller was.

Gideon keeps his eyes on the road as he finishes, "Sam gave me a time to meet her on the message, but she never showed. I got worried so I sent Tucker to check on her. When he got there the police where everywhere. Both Tucker and I worried that if this person attacked Sam at her home, then he know where she lives and likely to know that she has a sister. We were worried he may attack you too. That was Sam's biggest fear."

Chapter 7

∞

Gideon and I pull into the parking lot at the hospital. Out of habit, I try to open the door again. I hate having to wait on Gideon to open the door. I step out into the cool late night air.

"Thank you, Gideon." I know I was very rude to him, it is not an excuse, but I am under a lot of stress

right now. I will tell you a secret; it felt great to be jumping on someone's ass. My shoulders feel lighter.

I wonder what time it is. I reach into my pocket for my cell phone, push the button on the side of my phone, and see that it is 1:27 am. Wow. It feels later than that to me. Maybe that is because I have lived a lifetime in the last few hours. Gideon did say he does not know who did this to Sam, but will find out. He also said he would be taking care of them himself. I shudder at the thought of what that means.

"Are you ready?"

I turn to reply to Gideon, "You don't have to go with me." I put my phone back in the pocket of my dress.

With a smirky smile he responds, "Oh yes I do," as he walks past me toward the hospital. I am standing in the parking lot stunned. "Are you coming? I am not leaving you alone so get over it Sarah." I chase after him because the parking lot is dark and scary; at least that is what I tell myself the reason is.

We are in the elevator when I proclaim, "I am sorry for the way I acted in your home."

Gideon does not say anything, just turns his head to look at me. Then out of nowhere, he leans into me bumping his shoulder into mine. It shocks me and I laugh out loud. I cover my face with my hand in embarrassment. When I succumb to moving my hand from my face, I do not move my head. I roll my eyes to look over at him, and then bump him back.

The elevator dings as we reach the floor of the ICU. "I wonder if they will let me see my sister again."

"Sarah, she needs her rest, and it is only a few hours until the first visit of the morning. You may need to wait until then."

I cross my arms and pout. I know he is right, but I really do not want him to be right.

Lola, my inner crazy girl, has her arms crossed too, but goes one-step further with the pouting. She has her tongue stuck out and is shaking her head from side to side. I giggle at myself. Gideon looks at me and tilts his head to one side, but does not say anything.

We step out of the elevator and again, I am in the waiting room of ICU. The man Tucker left here to stay with Sam stands when he sees us. Gideon crosses in front of me to meet; oh, I forget his name.

"Mr. Glass, what are you doing here?" He reaches up to his

loosened tie, fumbling to tighten it back up. He looks confused.

As Gideon is walking over to... well, it will come to me in a minute, he says, "Mister Adams, I brought Ms. Wilds to be with her sister."

That is right. That is his name. Mr. Adams.

Gideon shakes Mr. Adams's hand. "Has Tucker been in touch with you?"

"Um, yes sir. He has called every hour to check on Ms. Sam Wilds."

Adams does not look Gideon in the eyes as they talk. I hate when people do not look you in the eyes when they speak to you, makes me feel like they have something to hide.

Gideon introduces us. "Mr. Adams, this is Sarah Wilds, Sam Wilds sister."

Mr. Adams puts out his hand out to shake mine. He looks me in the eyes with a glimpse of a tender heart, but he still throws me off for some reason. I cannot put my finger on why.

Looking at Mr. Adams, he is an overly tall, thin man. His skin is very pale, and he wears a crew cut hairstyle; black hair. Mr. Adams has small beady eyes that look like lasers staring a hole through you if you look at him to long. His smile is slimy, and he just unnerves me.

"Ms. Wilds, I am taking all precautions to keep your sister safe, I want you to know that."

I look at him for a blink before responding. "Well that is great. I *hope you will keep her safe." What do you say when someone tells you they will take all precautions to keep your sister safe? I pull my hand from his and walk toward the door to where Sam is lying in a bed, in a coma.*

I begin to wonder if Mr. Adams really will keep Sam safe. Who is this guy? I may need to be asking myself who is Gideon Glass. I am putting all my trust in these people, and I have no idea who they are.

Sam was always quiet about her work. Most of the time I would be thankful for that, but right now I am wishing I would have been a little more involved. She owns two strip clubs and I find out, through someone else, she has a silent partner in one of them who is a strong-arm guy. Gideon does not seem like the type of guy that would let someone cross him, and if they try, I am not sure they would live to tell about it.

I touch the door that opens to the ICU. The nurses will not let me *in yet so I walk over to a chair sitting by the ICU door and plop my tired body into it.   Gideon and precautionary guy are on the other side of the room talking. Mr. Adams has his back to me. Gideon looks up and smiles at me when he sees me sit in the chair. I lean my head back on the wall and pull my feet up in the chair with me.   Gideon touches Mr. Adams on the shoulder before he walks over to me. Mr. Adams sits in front of the television again, and before I close my eyes, I see him pick*

up the newspaper Tucker had left
earlier.

I open one eye to look at
Gideon while he talks. "Sarah, that
does not look like it can be
comfortable. The way you are
sitting, that is."

"Well right now it is as good as
it gets."

"You could be sleeping in a
warm bed at my house right now if
you would have stayed," he says as
he sits in the chair next to me.

"This is really where I need to
be. But you are not a prisoner here.

You can go to your house and sleep whenever you get ready. I will be alright."

Gideon looks at me for a second with that smirky smile before he says, "I told you I am not leaving you alone. Some crazy man attacked your sister. We don't know if he will attack you too or not."

I hit my hand on my leg as I look at him and say, "What the heck are you talking about? All you are doing is scaring me. Yes, someone attacked my sister. That does not mean they are going to get me, and if they do I can hold my own. By the way, who made you my automatic protector when my sister got hurt? Why are you so hell bent on finding out who did this? What is in it for you? Besides Mr. Glass, I am a grown woman and I can take of myself."

I stand up and head toward the elevator. I want out of here. I want out of here now. I want to get away from Gideon. I want to get away from Mr. Adams. I would most like to run and hide in a closet somewhere. I cannot breathe. My throat is closing as the walls of the waiting room are closing in.

I decide to bypass the elevator. I see the door with the universal sign for stairs. I run to the door and push it hard enough it flies into the wall behind it. I sprint down the three flights of stairs. As I am watching the steps and running, I can hear Gideon with Mr. Adams. They are yelling at me and at each other. I do not hear what they are saying, and I do not care. I just keep running. I need out of here and away from them.

When I reach the lobby floor, my legs are like jello. I hit the door hard with my body. The door flies open and I fall out into the lobby still hanging on the door as my knees scrape across the floor. Dang that hurts. But I do not care. I have to keep running.

"Come on! Keep going! We can get away; just keep running!" Lola continues to cheer and I continue to listen to her voice in my ear.

I look around to find the main entrance. Thankfully, it is right in front of me. I run to it, take a deep breath, and head out into the courtyard of the hospital. I turn toward the vast parking areas and sprint to find my car.

My car is at the back of the parking lot, and all I can think is, "So why do I park at the back of a parking lot again?" Nevertheless, I can see it.

As I am running, I can hear Gideon yelling. I think he is talking to Mr. Adams. He is too far away for me to understand what he is saying. Right now, all I can hear is my heart pounding in my ears and the steady breathing I am doing. I run every day. For me it is my release of all my sins, my drama, and myself.

My eyes are on my car when suddenly, I hear tires squeal to one side of me. I stop immediately to see where the noise is coming from. I can see headlights. I think to myself, "Oh crap, those head lights are heading right for me." Hear

Gideon yelling "run Sarah," *instead of turning and running away, I turn and run right toward the car. The only thing on my mind now is Sam. This has to be the person who has hurt her. I want to see if I can see him. I am not thinking about the fact that this is a car coming toward me. I am thinking I want to see his face. I thought I wanted to see it for Sam, but I think it is more for me. I just have to remember to move when he gets close to me. I can do this. Here comes the car. Keep your* eyes on the driver. JUMP! JUMP NOW!

It works! Right before the car is too close, I jump to one side and roll like cat woman through the parking lot. I remembered to keep looking at the car so I would possibly get a good look at him.

Chapter 8

∞

Again, I can hear Gideon yelling. I think he is yelling at me. I try to pick myself up off the parking lot; everything in my body hurts. My head is swimming. I turn to find my car again. I stumble backwards a few steps before fumbling forward. I can see my car. I start to run again, everything is pulling and creaking. What was I thinking? All I wanted to do is see his face. Running toward a moving car was stupid. As I make my way toward my car, I look behind me and see Gideon. He is catching up to me, but maybe I can get to my car before he gets to me.

I reach my car, get my keys out of my pocket, and put them in my hand. I come up on my car with one shot. I hit the hole to unlock the *driver side door. I jump in, slam the door, and punch the keys in the ignition all in one motion. I am shaking from the adrenaline rushing through my body. Gideon hits the window and opens the door at the same time. He grabs the keys out of the ignition. I slam my hands on the steering wheel repeatedly, then put my head down on the steering wheel in defeat, and let out all my adrenaline, my fears, and my tears once again.*

Gideon laces his arms around me. He leans me into his body so I am crying on his shoulder. I am sobbing so hard that I cannot catch my breath. Gideon is rocking slightly side to side. If I was a baby, I think he would be singing my tears away right now.

All of the sudden I stop crying, jerk my head up, and look him in the eyes with distain, but my distain is not for him.

"Where is the bastard that tried to run me over?" I say as I push Gideon away from me. Accidently

knocking him off balance, I jump out of the car like a little bandy rooster.

Gideon is sitting on the ground as he says, "Sarah he drove off. Steve is going after him now in his car."

I wheel around to look at him, "Who is Steven?"

Gideon smiles as he says, "Steve is Mr. Adams."

I stand in the middle of the parking lot for a minute with my hands crossed over each other while they rest on top of my head. All the color and feeling drains out of my body when I realize I ran toward a car. I fall to my knees for no other reason than my poor tired legs giving out on me.

"What on earth was I thinking? I think I have gone crazy."

Gideon is standing in front of me. I jerk my head up to look at him when he speaks.

"I think you have a lot to take in right now, and a lot has happened in a short time. That does not make you crazy. You are just having a *break from all that has happened to you." He kneels down and gets on his knees with me.*

My life has changed in the blink of an eye. My sister has someone who is trying to hurt her, if not kill her. Why is that? Then, the same person who is out to harm Sam tried to run me over. I just met her "silent partner" and still do not know who he really is. Is Gideon Sam's boyfriend? Or are they really just business partners? My heart sinks at the thought of him being

Sam's boyfriend. I shake my head to end the thoughts because right now that is the last worry I need to be having.

Hold the phone. I just remembered I got a short look at the man. I look at Gideon as I push myself up from the parking lot and stand one more time.

"I got a look at the guy. I got a look at the guy!" I bounce toward him and jump into his arms as I say it again, "I got a look at him. I cannot tell you a lot, but I did see him. That is why I ran toward the

car; I wanted to see if I could see his face."

Gideon jumps up off the ground just as excited. "Are you kidding me? I need to call Tucker!" He picks up the phone, starts talking, and then he looks at me. "Well, what did you see?"

I hit his shoulder with the back of my hand, "Oh yeah! Well, he was wearing a black cap. He was a white man, and had a school jacket on, like a letterman's jacket." I am walking in a circle with my hands on top of my head trying to think of other details. "But I can't see what school it is! I think it was maybe red and white, or red and yellow?" I am pacing back and forth now in front of Gideon thinking. Finally, "I can see dark hair."

Gideon grabs me abruptly and pulls me into his body. "Look, I know you don't want to hear this but you are punchy and all over the place. You cannot remember his face because you are thinking on no sleep. You need to relax and calm your mind. It is late and your brain *is tired. Your sister needs you working on all cylinders."*

I think about it for a second as I look at him. Maybe he is right. I am all over the place. "OK. I will agree with you this time. I do need sleep. Sleep to help my sister. Now I need to find a bed."

Gideon grins still holding me tight in his grasp. "I think I can find you a bed."

All of the sudden my body heats up, hot enough to make me forget it is cold outside. I flush all over, at the thought of Gideon finding me a bed. My head tilts automatically when I think of Gideon in that bed with me.

Chapter 9

∞

The ride to Gideon's house is a blur. I have my head propped on my arm, my arm is propped on the passenger side window, and my eyes are closed.

"I love your car," Gideon says, as most people do. Gideon laughs when I tell him I have never owned

another car. He would not let me drive. It was hard letting him drive my car, but I am so tired I cannot fight. Reluctantly, I give him the key. I hate to let other people drive my car, but in this case, he could be right. I have been a little crazy.

This drama with my sister has made me crazy. It upsets me to think something like this has happened to us as a family again. I remove my head from the comfort of my arm, prop my arm on the door rest, and look out the window as we drive in silence.

I lean my head back on the headrest, and close my eyes again. I will the memory of my parent's death to flood over me. Sam and I were young when we lost our parents. Remembering their death is the only way I can see them anymore, and right now, I need to see them.

I can see Lola is in the corner of my head, curled up in a ball in her tee shirt and a pair of panties. She knows where we are going, and she hates this place.

"I need them, Lola."

She shakes her head with tears in her eyes. I talk to her as if she is another person. It feels good to have her to talk to sometimes. I do not know how long she has been with me; I believe she showed up when my parents died. I cannot remember her before that, but I cannot remember a lot before that. I feel like she helps me stay sane sometimes.

We pull up to the house just as my mind begins to drift back in time. Interrupting my thoughts,

Gideon brings me back to this century, "Well Sarah, we are back where you and I met."

I look at him tiredly and reply in a quiet voice, "Yes Gideon, we are."

Lola is whipping her head with the back of her hand. She knows she is off the hook for now, but I need my parents so they are coming.

I step out of the car while Tucker holds the door open for me. He can tell I am zapped I guess because he does not even look at me, nor does he say anything. Gideon comes over to my side of the car and puts out his arm for me to grab it. I think for a second I am going to push past him, but his arm looks so inviting and I am not sure I can walk without assistance. All the adrenaline is gone from my body now and pain fills in where the adrenaline once existed.

Gideon walks me up the stairs and inside the still lit dwelling, just as we left it. We walk through the door and he grabs me by the hand saying, "Let me show you the room that Mrs. Tucker has made up for you." I smile and walk with Gideon hand in hand up the stairs where he shows me to a room that is much better mannered than the rest of the house.

The room is rather large. There is a calming effect to it, maybe it is the warm color painted on the walls. It is a milk chocolate color. The bedding is sky blue, and makes me want to fall in it and die. The furniture in the room is sparse. There is one small dresser with four drawers at the other side of the room, and two nightstands on either side of the bed.

I am standing in the middle of the room not moving or saying anything. Gideon finally speaks up.

"So what do you think, Sarah?"

"Gideon, it is very unlike the rest of your house."

"I know. Before Stan and Rachel married this was where she stayed. Stan and Rachel married about two years ago and I decided to build them a house down the driveway."

"Who are Stan and Rachel?"

"Mr. and Mrs. Tucker."

"Oh OK. That is why it seems more girlie."

"Well I thought she needed her own space so I let her do what she wanted to in here."

"She has great taste."

I sit on the bed next to Gideon. We sit in silence for a few minutes.

"I guess I will leave you so you can get some sleep."

"You're right. I am a little tired. I will see you in the morning. Or should I say soon?"

Gideon stands, turns back to me as he is walking out of the room, and says, "Yes, Sarah, you will see me soon." He smiles and looks down at the floor as he shuts the door.

I fall back onto the bed laying there for a moment staring at the ceiling not thinking of anything. And then, I feel myself finally falling asleep. I am drifting out of this world and into a world where I find *my mother just as I left her the moment she left Sam and I.*

I am eight years old again standing in the hallway of the house I live in now. I can see into the living room. On the other side of the living room is my mom. She looks like she fell asleep. As I look at her, I wonder how she fell asleep like that. She is sitting in a chair in front of the fireplace. Mom's body is slouched precariously, and her hair is in her face. Her arms are behind her, it seems something is holding her body to the chair.

I call out to her from the hallway, "Mom! Hey, Mom!"

She is motionless. I move my legs toward her. I pass the couch to get to her. Passing the couch, I see something out of the corner of my eye. I turn my head toward what is there. It is my dad. He is also in one of the dining room chairs. The chair is lying on its side. His hands remain tied behind his back to the chair. I wander over to him, drop to my knees, and shake him.

"Dad, what is wrong with you? Wake up, Dad." His body is cold under my fingers. "Dad, please wake up." Tears are flowing down my face now. I scream at mom, "Mom! Wake up!"

I pull myself up off the floor and walk over to my mom. I lift her head. It is heavy, and she is so cold. All I can do now is scream.

Once my screams stop, I am lying on the floor in the living room between my dead parents. For some reason my mind is foggy. This is a weird feeling. I sit up as I hear a noise behind me. My heart is pounding out of my chest, and then suddenly I see Sam stumble out of the shadows of the hallway.

I jump up onto my feet and run to meet Sam before she sees what I saw. I want to tell her what happened, but I do not want her to see it. Quickly, I turn Sam around and lead her back to the kitchen.

After her initial shock of me dragging her into the kitchen, Sam looks at me and says, "Rosebud, *what is wrong with you? And why have you been crying?"*

I try to keep it together, but after she called me Rosebud, I lost it. I burst into tears, "They are dead, Sam. They are both dead."

Frantically, Sam shakes me. "What are you talking about? Who is dead?"

I collapse into her body as I answer, "Mom and Dad. Sam, Mom, and Dad are dead."

Sam's body gives way and we both wilt to the floor. Sam is rubbing my hair as she rocks me and cries. All she can say is, "Shh. Don't cry, Rosebud. We will make it through this."

I want to believe her, but right now, all I am thinking is here she and I sit, and we are all we have.

I lift my head off Sam and push myself up off the floor once more. I walk over to the phone and dial 911. The dispatcher answers the phone and my voice cracks, "We need help at 212 Briar Grove."

"Why sure, Honey. You want to tell me what happened?"

"Yes Ma'am. Both of my parents are dead," the phone goes silent.

Sam and I are both in the back of an ambulance. There are people everywhere. Two emergency workers are in the ambulance with us looking Sam and I over.

"I think these two girls were drugged," one of the workers says as they make us follow a light being shined in our eyes.

"Well, that would explain why they didn't hear or see anything."

Sam looks over at me. She grabs my hand. "We are going to be OK, Rosebud."

I grin as tears roll down my face, and I think both of the men realize how callus they are being.

Rosebud was a name given to me by our Dad. I do not know why he called me that. He called Sam, Cherry Blossom. We never seemed to ask why he called us that. And we still do not know to this day. However, we still call each other those names, but we do not allow anyone else to use them.

Chapter 10

∞

My eyes fly open and my upper body bolts off the bed. I grasp for air while grabbing at my chest, sweat rolling off my body. I am coughing trying to catch my breath when the door to the bedroom flies open. I look up panicked to find Gideon running

towards me and Mr. Tucker behind him with his gun pointed in the room. I try to talk, but I cannot seem to catch my breath.

Gideon sits next to me on the bed. When they realize nothing bad is happening, he grabs me. But I wave him off and shake my head at him. I am fighting to get air right now, the last thing I need is someone holding me. He gets up from the bed and stands in front of me.

"Sarah, what do you want me to do? Can I get you some water?"

I shake my head again at him. I close my eyes and grab my heart as tight as I can. I feel my body starting to loosen and the net around my lungs starts to release. I have asthma, and sometimes fear brings it on. I can breathe again. I close my eyes and take in air, beautiful oxygen infused air.

Gideon sits back down. Sarah, you scared me. Are you sure you're alright?"

I shake my head no. I am still fighting to breathe, and I do not want to waste air talking right now.

I have a rescue inhaler, but of course, I left it at home. I will never leave home without it again. When I was a child, Aunt Lela would make me lift my arms over my head. Out of habit, I lift my arms up over my head. I may look stupid, but this really helps most of the time.

Tucker has put the gun down finally. He is still looking around the room when Gideon reassures him that everything is OK. Tucker *turns to Gideon, nods, and steps out of the room, closing the door behind him.*

Gideon looks back at me, eyes glassed over from being asleep. I cannot bring myself to look at him yet. I am excessively embarrassed. I think to myself, how he knew I was in distress is beyond me. He must have cameras in the room. That would not surprise me at this point in my knowledge of Gideon. He is very cautious and guarded. I can admire that though, I am that way too. The guarded part of him intrigues me, but the kind side makes me long for him.

When you look at Gideon, you do not think of kindness. His armored exterior screams gladiator. That is what I really thought when I first met him. Nevertheless, there is a warm soul behind all that armor, and that soul is making me yearn for him.

I build the courage up to look at him. When I do look up, he is staring at me. There is not a muscle moving on his body. I stare back at *him. I am the first to release the stare when I realize Gideon is shirtless.*

My eyes wander down to his bulky bare chest. He has freckles. I really want to touch them. I lift my hand off the bed and cautiously start moving my hand towards his chest. I can see his breathing quickens. I close my eyes and glide my fingers along the ripples of his stomach.

Gideon startles me, and out of fear, I retract my hand. In his raspy, molten lava deep voice, he questions me. "Sarah, what happened? I heard you screaming. Hell, your screams were so loud; Tucker heard them at his house. I was about to call him when he busted through the door, guns blazing because he heard your screams too."

My eyes lock onto his when I hear I was screaming. "I was screaming? I am so sorry. I didn't mean to wake everyone."

Gideon touched my face with his hand. "Why did you scream

Sarah? What scared you that bad? Was it just a bad dream?"

"You could say it was a bad dream." I pull my face out of Gideon's gentle grip and push my body off the bed to get away from the heat swelling inside me. "Gideon, I am sorry about waking everyone. I have bad dreams sometimes and they seem to pop up when I get stressed." I did not want to tell him I willed the nightmare to happen.

I am still facing away from him when I feel the heat rising in me again. I know he must be standing behind me now. I stand there for a moment, close my eyes, and pray for him to touch me. A small part of me is thankful when he does not.

I like the feeling he gives me when he is so close, but I must push that feeling aside. He is more than likely taken, and my luck would be that woman being my sister.

I quickly pat the pockets of my dress looking for my cell phone. It is not there. It must have fallen out onto the bed. I turn around to look on the bed; I must know what time it is. I need to go to my shop and leave a note for people coming by.

Gideon laughs, "Is this what you're looking for?"

"Yes. I need to know what time it is." I grab the phone from his hand as I cock my head to one side with a smirky smile and say, "Thank you."

It is 5:49. That should be enough time to get to the shop and get out before anyone sees me. I look at Gideon who is now standing in the doorway of my room, or his room that I am using.

"I bet you need to go to your shop From House to Home, right?"

I want to ask him how he knows that, but I just do not have the time.

"Yes, I do. I have to leave a note for my clients even though I am sure the whole town knows what happened to Sam by now. I just need to leave a notice on my door."

Gideon looks at his watch and responds, "Give me five minutes and

I will go with you. Let me call Tucker to drive."

"You don't have to do that. I can go by myself, or Tucker can drive me."

Gideon pays no attention to me and just smiles and walks out of the room. Down the hallway from me he replies, "I will be going with you, and that is that Ms. Wilds."

I stomp my foot on the ground in silent protest.

Sitting on her couch, Lola is laughing at me. She points her finger at me and begins to sing, "Sarah has a crush. Sarah has a crush." Sometimes I wish I could slap her.

I am in the living room of Gideon's house, standing at the glass walls watching the sunrise on the property surrounding the house. If I were not so gloomy this would be a beautiful morning. I hate I am missing the first visits with Sam, but I have to do this first. I hope she does not realize I am not there yet.

Tucker opens the front door at the same time Gideon is entering the *room. So do they plan these things? Gideon heads towards the front door. When he gets there, he holds the door open and waves his hand at me. "After you, Ms. Wilds."*

Gideon and I exit the house with Tucker following right behind us. The car is running in the driveway. Gideon opens the door for me and I slide into the back seat. For some reason I am nervous about this ride.

Chapter 11

∞

Gideon and I are in the back seat of his sporty SUV. I am looking out the window on one side with my arm propped on the door rest. Every so often, I glance over at him. He is motionless as he looks out the other window. I wonder what he is thinking. I know what I am thinking, about the moment we shared together and how I would love to share a moment like that with him again.

As I stare out the window, I watch the sun cast shadows onto the road. It looks like the shadows are dancing a waltz as we drive by, swirling around behind us. I look out across a field we are passing, and the sun is glistening off the frost that has kissed everything exposed to it. I have always loved watching the sun come up. If ever there was a more beautiful moment, God kept it for himself.

All I can think about is the night I have endured, all that has happened, all I have learned, and where all of it will lead me. I think back to when I ran at the car and saw the letterman jacket he was wearing/ was it red and white, or red and yellow. There was something on the sleeve of the jacket. Out of habit, I close my eyes to think of it. Class of 2003 was the badge. Class of 2003. That is the same year Sam and I graduated.

My arm falls off the door rest and I bump my head on the window. Wait! Wait! A red and white jacket with a class of 2003 badge that is the same colors of Hollow Springs High School. Please do not tell me it is someone we know?

"Sarah, what is wrong? Are you OK?"

"I remember the letterman jacket had a badge on the sleeve. It was a class of 2003 badge."

One corner of Gideon's mouth went up in a smirk before he said,

"OK that is great! Do you remember what color the jacket was?"

"Yes. It was red and white. Gideon you know what the worst part is? Those are the same colors of Hollow Springs High School, and 2003 is the year Sam and I graduated."

Gideon's mouth dropped as did mine when I said it out loud. I looked into the rearview mirror. Tucker is looking at me. He has not said a word. I wonder what he is thinking right now. By the look on *his face, I am thinking Tucker has murder on his mind.*

Gideon leans his head back on the headrest. "Well, that will narrow down our search, right Tucker?"

"Yes sir. That will narrow it way down."

I know Gideon and Tucker are happy the list is smaller, but me not so much. Fact of the matter is the list is narrowed down to everyone I grew up with.

My mind is elsewhere when I realize we are at my shop. I reach to open the door, but this time I stop myself. I am finally remembering the door is not going to open. Gideon opens the door for me after Tucker lets him out. I look up at him as he waits for me to get out.

"I remembered the door lock this time."

Gideon laughs. "That just means you are figuring out my tricks."

I smile at him, but say nothing even though he is right. I am starting to figure him out somewhat.

I walk toward the front door of my shop to open it when I hear a shrill southern voice, "Why Sarah Wilds. What on Earth, are you doing young lady? And Honey, who are these strapping men you have with you?"

I turn toward the voice even though I know exactly who it is. "Mrs. Trapper. What are you doing out this early in the morning?"

I took a deep breath as I saw her walking this way. I knew she was the last person I wanted to run into this early.

Mrs. Trapper saunters up the steps of my shop, "I take my daily walk this time every day." She leans her head to one side and smiles that big Texas girl smile. However, I know what is about to happen. The interrogation is about to begin.

Then I give her my big Texas girl smile back as I say, "OH! I had no idea you walked in the morning."

"Yes. It gets my old blood pumping."

I have smiled so much my face hurts. So this time I simply say, "I was just going to leave a note on the door, letting people know I would not be in today or tomorrow." I was hoping that would head her off, but to no avail.

Mrs. Trapper steps under the awning that covers the front door. She tilts her head to one side and looks me with concern. Mrs. Trapper is a good woman, but like most southern women, she is nosey.

"Oh yes, I heard about Sam. That is just awful. What happened, Honey?"

I put my head down as I decide whether to answer her question or not.

Then, without a thought, Mrs. Trapper says, "Well we all know what happened."

I lift my head up to look at her, because I want to hear what she has to say next. "It was Sam's business choice that finally caught up to her." She leans in to add just a little more,

"Are they sure this was an isolated incident?"

I lean my head back and close my eyes as I think to myself, she means no harm. Killing her will only get you in trouble. Bunny is just Bunny. She really drives me crazy sometimes though, and she forgets to think before she speaks.

Lola has on boxing gloves. She is bouncing around a boxing ring punching at the air and shuffling her feet. "Please let me hit her!"

I laugh at Lola but really, Bunny is just Bunny.

I am thinking of how to reply to Bunny when I hear Gideon say to her, "Mrs. Trapper, let me introduce myself. I am Gideon Glass." He leans in to her and she turns to meet his gaze as he finished her off with words, "I don't think you have anything to worry about. It's Mrs. Trapper, right?" He does not wait for her to answer and continues talking, "We do think it is an isolated incident." Gideon then grabs Mrs.

Trapper's hand and starts to lead her back to the sidewalk.

Gideon is still talking to her as they walk away. I cannot hear what they are saying until I finally hear Bunny say, "OK! Sarah, you take care of Sam. I will check periodically on your shop and your house. I will call you if there is anything strange going on." Then she starts back on her morning walk.

Chapter 12

∞

Gideon walks back to the door as Tucker and I are walking in. I look at him when I open the door to let him go in before me. I cannot help myself; I have to ask, "So what did you say to her?"

He turns to me as I close the door. "I just told her she had nothing to worry about. We thought it was an isolated incident, and even if it wasn't an isolated incident she would not be a target." Gideon smirked at me when he said that. I shake my head at him knowing what he is really saying. He is really telling Mrs. Trapper that she is too old to be a target. "I also let her know you needed help right now, and I just asked her if she could check on things for you and let you know if anything suspicious is going on."

I look at Gideon with envy. He handled Mrs. Trapper like a pro. She did not even know what hit her. I know he is a hard ass, but all I've seen about him is kindness. I hope I don't miss my chance to see the kind side of Gideon Glass, instead of the mean side. I may like to see that side of him.

The three of us walk into the store together. I take a deep breath because I am finally home. I can smell the specialty candles I sell. I love the look of From House to Home and the smell when you walk in. There is a little bit of everything here. I like to draw people in so they want to shop all day. I carry large items like beautiful full-length mirrors, as well as small items like my favorite whimsical salt and peppershakers. The sunlight looks inviting when it beams through the storefront windows and around the glass shelves of the shop. At certain times of the day, you can watch the prisms dance around the store. It reminds me of little fairies fluttering about.

While we are at the shop, I decide to go ahead and grab a few things like my flash drive of accounts, my laptop, and a few things I can work on while Sam is in the hospital. I need to balance my books and get them up to date. This will be a good time to do that.

I find a marker, and grab a piece of paper from the printer. I am writing the note for my door when I look up and find Charlie Rhodes walking into my shop wearing a Hallow Springs letterman jacket. My mouth dries and I choke when I see him. The letterman jacket is red and white with a two thousand three badge on the sleeve. My stomach does a back flip into my heart. The shock on my face must radiate to Charlie.

"What?"

I look toward Gideon and Tucker. Gideon has his hand behind his back, and Tucker has his hand in his jacket. I know Tucker carries a weapon, it never crossed my mind that Gideon would, but his hand behind his back says he does.

The thought of both of them shooting Charlie pushes me into action, I shimmy around the desk in front of Charlie, and I grab his arm to lead him back out the door. I really want to throw him out on to the sidewalk, but I cannot condemn him just for wearing his letterman's jacket. There is no way he would do this to Sam, and he would never try to run me over with a car.

This is crazy to think! Charlie. The same guy that just helped my sister. I don't think he would hurt her, and then help her, right.

Although there are those people who do that, they hurt people to be their savior too. I wonder to myself what are those people called. I shake my head to bring myself back to reality. Who cares, right now this is Charlie. Charlie would never do this, no way.

I am standing there with Charlie while thinking through all of this. First, I am trying to wrap my head around the fact that Charlie is wearing a letterman's jacket. Second, this might be the guy who hurt Sam, and tried to run me over.

Charlie stops my thought process. "Sarah, what is going on? Are you OK? You look like you just saw a ghost." He grabs my hand while standing in front of me. I see movement out of the corner of my eye. I shake my head no. I can see Tucker reaching up to push the door open.

"Oh. I'm so sorry. Please forgive me. What can I do for you, Charlie? Why are you here?" I remove my hand from his grasp.

"I was driving to the coffee shop. I saw your lights were on so I

thought either you were here, or someone was here that didn't need to be."

I push a stray hair behind my ear, and look at the ground. "Thank you, Charlie, for checking on me, but I am fine."

Charlie puts his hands in his pockets and rocks back and forth on his heels shrugging his shoulders. "How is Sam doing?"

I touch his arm as I say. "Sam is still holding her own." I try to say that with a smile but cannot muster one and add, "She had to have surgery last night, and a blood transfusion. They have her in a coma still." I push through the pain of telling the story. "I have not heard any news so I am guessing that is a good thing." I look around as I finish, "I came to the shop to leave a note for my clients and get a few things."

Charlie looks in the window. Gideon and Tucker are glued to it like kids on a snow day. Then he looks at me and the inevitable is brought up, "Sarah, who are these guys? And are you sure you're OK?"

I look at him funny for a moment. Then I realize he is worried about my well-being. "Oh these two. They are, um, bodyguards. Sam had called one of them before. Whoever hurt her came to the house. Sam told Gideon she knew who was threatening her."

Charlie looks concerned. He begins to stutter, "Was she able to tell them who it was?"

I try to gauge Charlie's face as he asked the question. There is nothing, a stonewall he is.

I hear Gideon open the door. "Sarah, we need to go so we can get to the hospital before the next visitation."

"I will see ya later, Charlie. I need to go."

He shakes his head as he walks away. I watch him as he turns around and says, "Hey Sarah, tell Sam I said to get better and soon."

"I will Charlie."

I did not tell him if Sam told Gideon, I wanted to see how he would respond. There was no reaction. I close my eyes and say a little prayer to myself. Please do not let Charlie be the one who hurt Sam.

I think back to all of us as kids, playing at his grandparents. I run through my memory bank to see if I can find any signs of him being that crazy. I cannot find anything that would make me think he would hurt Sam. Maybe it is just a coincidence, him wearing that letterman jacket.

Charlie walks over to his car; he looks back at me and waves. I wave back as I walk back into the shop.

Gideon stands in front of me when I walk through the door. "I don't like that guy," he says. I turn my nose up, and just walk past him. I am not responding to that. He is Charlie. Poetry writing, lifesaving, soft-spoken, Charlie. He could not hurt a fly, right.

I pack the rest of the things I need from here and head out to the car. As I put my laptop and bag in the SUV along with a few other *things, I look around the town that's in front of me. People are walking by and waving. I wave back, and think to myself that some of these people are suspects. Someone in this town, the town that I grew up in, is out to get my family and maybe me. How can this happen? What did we do?*

I feel someone looking at me. I look around the streets and see Lane Carson sitting in his cruiser watching me. I raise my hand up to wave at him, but he doesn't respond.

He just drives off. Man, he is weird. I could see him doing something like hurting Sam. No, wait. He is a cop. He wouldn't do anything like that either. He grew up here too. There is no way.

I shake my head as I try to wrap my brain around the fact that someone in my town is now my enemy.

Chapter 13

∞

Gideon and I are in the SUV again, on our way to the hospital. We are both in the back seat. He is staring out the window with a scowl on his face. I cannot stand it anymore. "Gideon, do you think Charlie could be the one that is doing this to Sam?"

Gideon waits for a minute to answer. I think he is trying to find a way to ease my mind. "Sarah, people will surprise you. I could see him wanting to harm her."

I think about what he just said. "Is there something you are not telling me, Mr. Glass?"

Gideon's eyes narrow at me. I see Tucker look at me in the rear view mirror. I sit up straight in my seat, knowing they must be hiding something. "Ok you two," I point my finger back and forth between the *both of them. "What is it y'all are hiding? I want you to tell me now."*

It takes a few minutes, but finally Gideon speaks up. "Sarah, Charlie is a frequent customer at both of Sam's places, and sometimes Tucker here has to throw him out. He gets a little belligerent."

My bottom jaw drops. I close my mouth so a fly can't get in. Then I tilt my head to one side. "You mean Charlie, the deacon of The First Baptist Church of Hollow Springs, the same Charlie that helps others." I tilt my head to the other side and point my finger at Gideon. "You are talking about a man that goes to the nursing home to play dominos with the ladies every Monday morning." I pause for a moment. "That Charlie is at strip clubs?"

"Yes Sarah, the same Charlie. Lane Carson is also a regular of Sam's Dreams 'n Genies club." Gideon points his finger back at me. "See, you would be surprised who shows up to 'these places'. Hell Sarah, some of the couples in your *tiny town grace the doors of at least one of the clubs, if not both of them."*

"What?! There is no way that happens. And who are some of these couples?"

Gideon smirks when he looks at me, "Well, Ms. Sarah Wilds, why don't we just go up there tonight and you can see for yourself?"

I gasp in disgust and throw my body into the seat. To make things worse, Gideon reveals that it is Friday night, and drinks are half price, which means this is when most people show their faces at the club.

"I am not sure I want to do that. I despise the thought of going in there. And what if the people from Hollow see me? What would they think of me in there as my sister lay in the hospital?" Oh, what am I thinking? There is no way I can go in there; the church would disown me.

Gideon laughs as he declares under his breath, "Most of your town is in there tonight anyway."

I scowl at Gideon. I do not condone what these clubs are all about. I have strong morals that our parents taught us. Besides, just because some of the people from Hollow Springs go does not make it OK for me to do as they do. I am a staple in the community.

We get to the hospital with minutes to spare before the second visitation. I speed walk through the parking lot so I can hurry and get to Sam, and I don't want someone running me down. I have walked so fast, that when I reach the main entry door I almost run into it. Gideon laughs at me again.

"You sure are finding it easy to laugh at me today." I roll my eyes at him and smile. I am still irritated at Gideon, but I find it hard to stay upset with him for some reason.

We are in the elevator and I am tapping my foot to the music when I realize I forgot to go by my house and get some things. "Well crap."

"Was that a curse word, Miss Wilds?"

I wheel my head around at him, "No."

"Oh, I thought you said crap. I was just wondering if that was your way of cursing."

I ram my shoulder into his arm and it knocks him off balance. I cover my mouth with my hand and chuckle to myself. He rolls his eyes at me and smiles.

"I forgot to go over to the house and get some things."

"You can't get into your house. And even if you could, you don't

want to right now. Tucker will go back to the house while you are here and get you what you need." Gideon then leans in closer than he ever has before, "Is there anything specific you need?"

My body is flushing as he still stands too close to me. "What I need is not at my house." I keep my head facing forward. I do roll my eyes over to look at him. He is staring at me. I bite my lip as I feel my body flushing all over.

Suddenly, Gideon turns to face me. I freeze, I am a little scared. He places one hand on the wall behind my head. He leans his body in to me with his face is so close I can feel his breath on my ear. I want to close my eyes, because that is my fire spot. I call it that because if you ever want to start a fire in me, you start at my ear.

"Maybe what you need is at my house." He moans a low moan in my ear. I almost melt into the floor of the elevator.

I am brought back to reality when the doors of the elevator open to the waiting room of ICU. There is no one in the waiting room at this time. The television is on and the news is echoing around the walls of the empty room. My knees are weak, but I step out of the elevator. Tucker is behind me. I wonder if he saw any of that. If he did, his face is giving nothing away.

The smells of the waiting room almost knock me down. It must be the memories it brings back from last night. I leave Gideon and Tucker watching the news as I head toward the door to the ICU.

The door opens and again I am in the maze of coordination. Last night Sam was the only person here. Today there are two more people. I walk past the nurses sitting at their stations. But don't bother to look at them. I keep my eyes on the curtain standing between Sam and I.

I pull the curtain back and there is Sam, just as I left her last night. She is still in a coma, and the machine is still breathing for her. I walk over to her bed, grab her hand and start to talk to her telling her what all has been going on. The nurse last night said she could hear me. I am going to hold on to that.

A new nurse comes in while I'm talking to Sam.

"Hello, my name is Lori. I am the day nurse that will be taking care of Samantha."

I smile at her but keep talking to Sam.

"May I ask who you are?"

"Yes, sorry. I am Sam's sister, Sarah."

"OK, great. I was told to keep records on who visits Samantha."

"Um, I didn't tell them to do that. Who ordered that?"

"Well maybe it was your parents?"

"No, no. It wasn't our parents. They are both deceased. I am her only living family and I did not order that."

She looks dis-shoveled as she grabs at the curtain, to find her way out. "I will see if there is any record of who ordered that."

"That would be nice."

I look through the curtains of Sam's little cubical and see Lori on the phone. She is a pretty thing with shiny long blonde hair that falls down her back even with it pulled up into a ponytail. She is tall and skinny, her uniform is a modern style that is form fitting. You can tell she more than likely works out. Maybe she is a runner. She can see me looking at her through the curtain. She gives me a small smile and turns her back to me. I get the feeling for some reason that phone call is about my sister, or me.

I turn back to Sam and whisper, "What the heck is going on here? Why someone would want to know, who is visiting you is beyond me? And who is this Lori girl?" I walk back over to Sam's bed to sit down next to her. All I can think about is someone is keeping tabs on my sister. When it's time to leave, I'll have to remember to ask Gideon about this.

A few minutes later Lori is back. "The person that wanted to know who came in Sam's room is

Officer Carson. Also, Ms. Wilds, the time is up for this hour. You can come back again the next hour. I believe the doctor should be in soon. Maybe we will have an update on Samantha when you come back."

I look at Sam not wanting to leave her here alone again. However, I know I have too.

"OK, Sam. I have to leave. I will return at the next hour. I love you Sam. See you soon." I give her a kiss on the forehead and start my walk out of the ICU when it hits me -

the nurse said Officer Carson, not Chief Carson.

I pivot around to find the nurse. We almost head butt each other as I run right into her. I grab her by the shoulders, to keep from losing my balance.

"Did you just say to me Officer Carson?"

"What? Oh, yes I did say Officer Carson."

"Not Chief Carson, right?"

You can tell she is getting frustrated with me, "I am not sure.

The chart says...," she pauses for a moment as she looks to confirm, "Officer Lane Carson."

I snap my fingers, "Thank you so much. You just told me what I needed to know."

I run out into the waiting room. When I open the door, I see Gideon talking to someone. I cannot tell who it is but I can see he is a police officer. I also see that Gideon is in his face and their conversation is heated. I head over to see what is going on. Suddenly, Gideon pushes the cop up against the wall. "Sarah, leave! Get out of here!"

I am at a standstill trying to process what is going on.

"Sarah, run! Leave! Get out of here, please!"

My feet move without me willing them to move.

Chapter 14

∞

I run past Gideon, getting a glimpse of whom he is holding. It is Lane Carson! I bolt toward the elevator as Lane shoves Gideon into me. Gideon and I both fall to the floor. He lands on top of me. Lane lunges forward with gun in hand. He points it at Gideon and me. Lane rears his leg back and kicks Gideon in the side with his steel toe boot. I wince in pain at the thought.

Lane grabs me by the hair and yanks me out from under the safety of Gideon's body. "Sarah Wilds, you are under arrest for the attempted murder of Samantha Wilds."

"You are crazy, you piece of," Lane kicks him again and Gideon is doubled over in pain.

Lane twists me around as he places handcuffs on me. Gideon jumps up off the floor. Lane pulls his gun out again and points it at me. "Don't make me have to shoot her." I scream "Gideon let him take me."

With my hands in cuffs, Lane leads me to the elevator. I look around searching for Tucker, but he is nowhere to be found. Where on earth is Tucker when you need him? Then I remember he was sent to my house to get some things that I had forgotten. Crap. He not being here is all my fault.

The elevator doors starts to shut when I hear Gideon yelling,

"Sarah, I will find you. Please don't worry. He needs you."

The doors shut. It is now Office Lane and me. He cackles a little to himself. I look at him, but do not say a word.

My only thoughts now are what Gideon said and the fact that again, I lied to my sister. I told her I would be at the next visitation. Standing here in handcuffs makes me aware that the next visitation is out of the question.

Lane leans into me and I cringe and try to pull away. "I am going to trust you not to run Sarah. Do you know why? That nurse you just met, she is my girlfriend, and she will kill your sister. And you know as badly as she has been beaten, no one will be any the wiser." I think to myself I knew I did not like that witch.

Lola is dressed as an Indian with a tomahawk in her hand and war paint on her face. She runs, screaming toward a wax statue of Officer Lane Carson to chop his *head off. I show no emotion, I just say thank you Lola.*

The elevator doors open, and like a good little prisoner I step out with my head high. There are three people standing outside the elevator doors. They eye me in disgust, but I really do not care. Lane walks out behind me with his hand on the cuffs and we head into the parking lot.

As Lane and I walk around the building across another parking lot,

I look for a way out. I must try to find a way out.

Then I realize even if I wanted to, I could not run. My hands are tight behind me. Officer Carson keeps me close. He also keeps reminding me of the nurse who has my sister. I can tell you, if that woman hurts or kills my sister, she will have me to deal with. And I am meaner than people think.

Lane reminds me again, of what she will do to my sister as he places me into the police car. I chuckle at him. "I don't know why *you are after my family, but I feel sorry for you."*

Abruptly, he slams my head into the doorframe of the car. I think it knocked me out cold for a second. I sit slumped over in the back seat of the car. I should stop talking but I cannot.

"So does it make you feel like a man to hit a woman with her hands cuffed behind her?"

He leans in the back door of the squad car. He is right in my face and my heart starts to pound. I know I cannot show any fear now. I don't move a muscle and I refuse to blink my eyes.

With breathy voice that smells of death and vodka, he begins, "You two bitch sisters are just like Carmen you never know when to shut up." My mouth drops at the mention of my mother's name.

You can see on Lane's face that he knows he has me off tilt. I was not expecting him to know my mother.

I think he was reading my mind when he speaks, "yeah I bet

you didn't know I knew your momma did you. Well Sarah I knew your momma well very well."

Pain builds in the back of my throat as Lane leans into me and smells my hair.

"You smell just like her."

I turn my head away from him and jam my shoulder into his chin as hard as I can.

Lane chuckles as he says "funny Sarah that was a good one you got me."

Tears are boiling to the surface I swallow them down to ask "Lane why are you doing this? What did we ever do to you?"

There is a long pause then Lane answers, "Sarah, I want you to know why I am doing this." I stare at him ready for the reason. Then he leans into me again and whispers "because Carmen, and James' deaths are coming back to haunt me."

For a moment my mind goes blank there is no thought at all. Suddenly, every thought I have ever had comes rushing to the forefront. I cannot process what he just said to me. The only words I can say are "those are my parents' names."

"Yes I know those are your parents' names. Lane steps out of the car. He places his hands on the hood of the car, he leans in close to me again "get with the program Grace, I killed your parents."

I sit straight up in the seat trying to get out of my handcuffs "why did you kill my parents you no good piece of."

Lane cuts me off *"don't you get it Carmen and I were in love, we were going to run off together, but your mom decided to stay with you girls and James."*

Lane leans his head down as if what he is about to say deflates him.

I look around hoping that maybe Gideon is close because we are still in the parking lot of the hospital, parked between the cafeteria and the main building. No one would think to look for us here.

I jump at the sound of Lane's voice, he is standing away from the *car now. He takes a long swig from a bottle he had hidden under the front seat.*

"I could not take Carmen, not wanting me and going about her life as if I didn't exist. I had thoughts of killing her and one night I decided to do it so I drugged you girls and killed them both."

I lean forward and heave bile all over the ground. I have heard all I can take. Lane does not stop; he just keeps talking about my parent deaths.

After we reliving the worst day of my life. He tells me recently he has been getting threatening letters from someone. He said the letters talked about what he did twenty years ago. One of the letters asking him if it was easy to kill, Lane said the letters wanted to know in detail how I killed the Wilds'.

My head spins and I do not know what is more torturing sitting in front of the man who killed your parents in handcuffs. Or listening to him tell you about their death and him being worried about threatening letters he received about it.

I am trying to listen to me sing to myself when Lane says, "I thought the letters came from Sam, so I decided I had to kill her too. But you foiled that plan."

I almost fainted when he said that. Therefore, he is the one who attacked Sam.

I made up the song I am singing to myself it is, "you just wait till I get out of these handcuffs. I am going to kill you." I sang it to myself repeatedly.

My brain starts working for a moment I remember him saying he thought Sam sent the letters. "What do you mean you thought it was Sam who sent you the letters? Was it?"

Lane looked at me "no it was not Sam who sent the letters. I got a letter this morning, but this letter told me what I needed to do to get back the evidence of your parent's death they have. The letter stated if I did what was asked of me I would *get all the evidence they have against me."*

I close my eyes, take a deep breath, and say "Lane what are you supposed to do?" I am pretty sure I know since I am sitting in the back of a police car in handcuffs, accused of attempted murder on my sister.

"I am to bring you to them. And if I don't they will take everything they have on me to the police. So Sarah I am going to do what I have to do."

All of the sudden the car starts to spin. I think he hit me with something. I can see the tunnel of darkness closing in, and without warning, the lights go out.

Chapter 15

∞

I try to open my eyes, but when I do my head pounds and my brain makes me close my eyes again. I can tell the car has stopped. I start to think maybe it is a good think I cannot open my eyes yet. I may not want to see where I am. I listen to see if I can hear voices, but hear nothing. I force my eyes to open. I am still in the squad car. What is going on? I lift my head up to look out the window. All I can see is a pasture on one side and the side of a building on the other. I think the building is a house. Lane parked the car on the side of the house. Where am I?

The only thing that is going through my mind is the one thing I learned in self-defense class; never let them take you to the second location. Here I am in the second location with a maniac that has beaten and almost killed my sister. Now what is he going to do with me?

All of the sudden I hear a man's voice yelling, "No! Stop! Please!"

I look out and see the window to the house is open. I see two figures struggling in the house. One of the figures pushes the other one away and reaches into his pocket. I am shocked as I see a gun and hear a shot! The flash from the gun makes me duck my head back down into the seat of the squad car.

I stay crouched in the back seat and realize I am alone here in the car. I sit up with my hands still cuffed behind my back. I wheel my body around to reach for the door handle and try to pull it. It does not budge. The pull lock on the door by the window is gone. Franticly, I pull on the door handle again. Nothing. There is Plexiglas between the front seat and me. I kick it out of anger.

I am trying to squeeze my hand out of the cuffs when I hear a screen door close. I stop what I am doing and duck down behind the front seat *and the Plexiglas. I see a figure of a man with a hooded sweatshirt on, but cannot see his face. He jumps off the porch of the house and heads toward the car. I scurry to the other side of the car and prepare for the fight that is coming. The door of the car opens and the hooded man bends down.*

I am lying in the seat on the other side of the car with both legs pulled into my chest. When the hooded man leans into the car, I kick both legs forward toward his face. He was ready for me. He grabs both my legs under one arm and holds them against his body. I am squirming trying to get away. The man leans into the car and pushes my legs back against my chest. There is nowhere for me to go, but that doesn't stop me from fighting. He reaches into the pocket of his hoody, "Fight Sarah, that excites me." His voice is dark but I recognize it.

He pulls a syringe out of his pocket. I keep squirming trying to get him off me. I know I am in trouble, my hands are cuffed behind my back, and he has my legs bound. I cannot get any force behind them. I want to scream, but I refuse to give him that satisfaction.

He puts the syringe in his mouth and removes the lid. I scream out in fear of what is in the syringe. He uses his free hand to push my face into the seat. He holds me there with his elbow. One side of my neck stands exposed to him. I know what is about to happen, I can feel the bile forming in my throat. I want to scream but just can't. I give in, close my eyes, and wait for the pain of the needle.

I feel his elbow move against my head. I squeeze the tears out of my eyes and the needle punctures my skin. My eyes open as the medicine burns going in. He pushes his body off me and I kick my legs at the air, but they fall to the seat below. I try to pick them up again. They do not move. I feel swimmy headed. The hooded man talks to me, but I cannot understand what he is saying. I keep trying to hold my *eyes open, eventually they fall closed, and my mind goes blank.*

Chapter 16

∞

I force my eyes open even through the pain. My whole body hurts. It feels like I have been in a fight. Then I remember I have been in a fight, for my life. I lift my body up to see where I am. I pat my chest to see if I am still dressed. I am. I look down at my clothes to see if they are mine and sigh in relief when they are. A prayer comes to mind, "Thank you, Lord," is all I say.

I need to look at my surroundings and remember where I am just in case I can get out of here. I need to be able to tell someone where the hooded man hid me. At least that is what happens in the movies, right?

I look around to see where I am. I am lying on a bed and wince at the pain as I try to lift myself up. Sitting on the side of the bed, I am woozy. I raise my hand to rub my forehead. It is heavier than normal so I look to see what is holding it down. My eyes fall on a shackle attached to my wrist. I wheel my body around through the pain.

I can see one of the nightstands have a chain resting on it. I pull at my arms and the chain moves. I follow the chain with my eyes. The chain ends at the bed. There is a second shackle attached to the bed frame. "Shoot me. You have got to be kidding me!" I look around the room, and back at the *chain and begin to realize this chain allows me to move around the room.*

On the other nightstand sits a plate of food. Really? Food? I am so not eating right now. A door stands on the other side of the room that appears to be to a bathroom. I stand and start to walk toward the bathroom. The chains will reach all the way to the toilet in the rear of the room.

I guess this is my prison. I sit back down on the bed and want to cry, but there are no tears. All I feel is anger. I want to claw Lane Carson's eyeballs out of their sockets with a heroin addict's spoon.

My heart starts to pound and I hear something in the distance. I lay back on the bed as if I have not moved at all.

The lock turns on the door and I quickly close my eyes. The door opens and someone comes to sit next to me on the bed. I really want to see who it is but I know I have to keep my eyes shut.

I do not want him to know I am awake. My lips want to curl up, *and bile slaps the back of my throat as I feel him stroke my hair. It takes everything I have in me not to roll away to the other side of the bed. I want to wrap this chain around his neck and choke him with it. I think he is the lowest scum that has ever touched this earth. All I really want is for him to leave, and stop touching me.*

He clears his throat, and he is still stroking my hair when he says, "Sarah, I'm sure you think I am a monster. I have always noticed that you keep your distance from me, but I have always watched you and wanted you." I recognize this voice. He keeps talking, "Your sister was as close as I could get to you most of the time. At least she would give me the time of day."

It takes everything in me to keep from saying there is a reason I would not give you the time of day. You are proving it now, because you are a sick fool. He stops stroking my hair but keeps his hand on my head.

"I would shop at From House to Home and you would keep to the back of the store until I was ready to check out. All I wanted from you was for you to talk to me."

I am lying as still as I can thinking this is a sorry ass who has a real funny way to show a girl that he likes her.

He keeps talking as he squeezes my head, "I have had enough of you ignoring me. I know you want to be with me, as I want to be with you. You can stop hiding it,

Sarah. I love you too." The voice is harsh and sweet at the same time. Every time he speaks, I am reminded of Sam lying on the floor of her bedroom, beaten.

I am about to crack and start screaming at him when I hear Gideon's voice ring in my head, "Sarah, I will find you." I wish he could hurry up and find me. All I can do is play here and wait to see if this guy will slip up so I can get out of here. I have to be strong. All my strength wants to rip his face off and spit in his eye sockets. What is *this man's problem? He is not living in the world; that is his problem.*

I can understand him fixating on Sam, but there is no way he should be fixating on me. I am no one. I am not the kind of person that gets stalkers. This cannot be happening to me. I have to get out of here, and soon, before he goes psycho.

Lane is sitting next to me. He has not spoken for a good while. I can tell he is still there. I can feel him on the bed, and I can smell his cologne heavy in the air. I do not know why, but it does not smell like Lane. Maybe this man is not Lane at all.

Finally, he gets up off the bed. I hear him sigh loudly before he says, "Sarah, you need to wake up. I want you to know how I feel about you and I am ready to tell you to your face." He places his hands on my shoulders it catches me off guard and I almost scream, but I bite my tongue instead. He shakes me violently, "Wake up, Sarah. I need you to wake up."

Oh my gosh! I just figured out the voice! It is not Lane at all! Charlie Rhodes is why I kept thinking about Sam lying on the floor. The voice is his!

I feel Charlie touch me again and I remind myself to stay limp as he keeps shaking me. I want to cry as he shakes me.

Abruptly he stops shaking me, and I hear him sigh and under his breath call me a bitch as he leaves the room. I wonder why he left. Oh well. I really don't care why he left.

I am just glad he did. I open my eyes. Now I can figure out a plan to get out of here.

First, I have to take care of my body fighting against me. In one motion, I jump off the bed, fly across the bedroom into the bathroom, and slide on my knees to the toilet. The bile that has built up in my stomach releases into the toilet. The bile is clear because there is no food in my stomach to expel. And, I will starve to death before I eat what he left me. I lay my head down on the toilet and start to concoct a plan to release myself from this sicko's grip.

I cannot believe he really thinks he is doing the right thing here. Keeping me captive is going to make me love him. Really, what is he thinking? Does he really think that I am that broken? Well he has messed with the wrong girl. I am going to remove this parasite from my life, and soon. I just have to come up with a plan to remove him.

I close my eyes and search my mind for Lola. Sometimes I need *her. For some reason she is nowhere to be found. She must be hiding somewhere.*

When I find her, she is dressed in camouflage from head to toe. She is blending into the background of a camouflage wall. Even her face is covered in camouflage paint. She has a machete in her hand and a smile on her face. She slices the air with her machete and places it back at her side before shouting, "Let's get this jack wagon!" A smile comes over my face as a plan comes to mind. Thank you, Lola.

Chapter 17

∞

I pick myself up off the bathroom floor and walk into my prison cell that resembles a bedroom. I stop at the opening of the bathroom door. There is someone in the room with me; I can feel them. I immediately look to one side of me. I see two windows. I could take my chances.

I bring myself back to reality when I look down and see the cuff around my wrist. I smile at the vision of me dangling off the side of the house. I close my eyes for a moment just to gather my thoughts before I grace him with a look.

Then I lift my head up, my eyes meet with the eyes of my capture, and a chill comes over my body when I see Charlie Rhodes. Someone I thought was a friend. He and I played as children. Did I distance myself from him, as I got older? Yes, maybe. His life went one way and mine went another. That is what I thought happened. I guess he thought I ignored him. We just became different people.

I almost cry at the thought of Charlie being the one who got my sister hurt. My plan has to be the same. The only difference is I am attacking Charlie Rhodes; someone I thought was a friend. I now need to know the answer to one question,

which only he can answer. Why
kidnap me?

"Why have you done this? I
thought we were friends?"

He looks at me for a moment
and does not say a word. There is a
kind, caring look in his eyes. Then
out of nowhere, the look of kindness
turns to anger or hatred. "Why
Sarah, all the years I have known
you, you have always acted like I
was a man with the plague. I never
knew you thought I was a friend."
He taps his finger on the bedpost
and adds, "I have shopped at your

store, and you make it a point to be in the back of the store the whole time I am in there. I hate to know that is how you treat your friends."

Charlie makes a move to come toward me I take a small step back. I can feel that I am up against the wall. He stops in his tracks and puts his arms out in front of him for a second before they fall back down to his side. Tears well in his eyes. "My intention is not to hurt you, Sarah."

My jaw drops. "What is your intention, Charlie?"

Charlie puts his head down looking a little defeated. When he raises his head he says, "Sarah, my intention is to have you all to myself." My heart pounds as I wonder if his plan is to keep me captive. There is silence between us when Charlie says in a childlike voice "I didn't know Lane would hurt Sam I am sorry for that. I never thought he would think Sam wrote the letters." he sighs as he finishes.

As Charlie looks down at the ground, I look around the room. My thoughts are all over the place. I *need him to come closer to me. I am going to have to let this man touch me if my plan is to work. I shudder at the thought but can hear Lola in my head, "Keep him talking, Sarah."*

My heart is pounding out of my chest and I feel my breathing is quickening. Deep breaths, I have to stay strong.

I have never seen this side of Charlie. He always seemed so put together. Today he is broken, and sad.

"So it was you who wrote those letters to Sam too."

There is a brief pause then Charlie screams, "I wanted Sam to figure out what Lane had done.

In a calmer voice Charlie adds "the letters to Sam where not meant to be threatening to her. I just told her things that happened the night of your parent's death."

I jerk my head up to look at him. I think for a second I want him to elaborate on that, but I decide not to ask. There is one thing I need to know.

"How did you know Lane killed our parents?"

"Well I happened up on that info by accident. I went to Lane's house a few months ago; we have become friendly over the years of working together. While I was there, I noticed a necklace above his fireplace with two rings next to them. I recognized the necklace first; I knew it was your mothers."

Charlie paced around the room as if he was recalling an old memory. "I thought I remembered seeing in the paper your mother's necklace and both, their wedding rings were missing from the scene. When I looked back at the old newspapers sure enough, there it was in black and white. I knew it had to be him."

Charlie stops and looks down at the floor "so one night I met him at the bar he had a few drinks no, a lot of drinks. So when I drove him home I questioned him. I had my phone on record and he spilled the entire store to me. In that moment I knew I had him, and I knew he would be the one to help me kidnap you."

I watch Charlie as he comes a little closer. He closes his eyes. Suddenly, he jerks his head to one side as if someone slapped him. But there is no one there.

I could fall apart at this moment. I could burst in tears and start crying but I cannot I have to be stronger than I have ever been. I close my eyes and pray. I pray for strength in the moment I attack Charlie. I pray I can attack Charlie.

He slowly starts walking around the bed toward me. I grip at the chain in my hand so tightly that it starts to throb. I am up against the wall as far as I can go. There is no turning back. I cannot wait until he gets close enough.

Charlie breaks my train of thought, "I know you will see I love you."

He moves a little closer, and I tighten my hands around the chain. I have to be patient. He has to come a little closer. I cannot lunge at him because he would then be able to stop me. I listen to him as he keeps talking about the night he drove Lane home. I want him to stop talking about it. I have learned so much about my parent's death today. I realize two people I grew up with are both pure evil.

After going into detail about my parents, Charlie says the one thing that moves me into action.

Charlie tells me my mother deserved what she got. When he said that, it took everything good inside me not to lunge toward him and wrap this chain around his neck.

For a second I thought I could just hope for the best. Instead, I took a deep breath and remembered I want to kill him. I do not want to give him a chance to kill me.

I beat the back of my head lightly on the wall. This is almost too much for me to hear.

Charlie keeps talking. "I kept trying to tell Sam about Lane but I could never find the words. So I started writing her letters just little poems. There were details about the *death of your parents and hints on who did it. I never meant for her to take it as a threat."*

Charlie paused for a second to rub his face with his hand. I wish he would get closer. I am losing my patients, I am about to try and lasso this chain around his neck and hope for the best. I close my eyes for a moment this time I pray for patients.

All I can think about is getting out of here. As Charlie paces the room away from me, I pray for him to come closer so I can get this over with. I want him dead. Now! It is all I can think about.

Charlie throws his head back and grabs his hair, "Sarah, all I want is for you to love me as I love you." He pounds his fist into his head as he talks.

I stare at him for a second, but I have to look away. I do not want him to see my fear. He takes a deep calming breath after the psychotic break he had.

"Sarah, I am ready to be with you, and love you. I understand it will take time for you to come *around, but you will stay here until you do."*

My mouth is wide open at what I just heard. I was right he wants to keep me here. "What do you mean? You will keep me here until I come around?"

Charlie grins, "You know you cannot leave. I finally have you."

He points his finger at me and says, "Lane told me he would get you here. But Sarah, I had no part in him taking you from the hospital, I promise." He throws his hands up in the air as if he is innocent. He keeps stepping a little closer. I watch him jump around like a bandy rooster as he tells me, "But don't worry. I took care of him. Lane can never hurt you again."

"Charlie, what did you do? Please don't tell me you did what I think you did."

Charlie steps a little closer. I want to strike, but not quite yet. He is not there yet.

"Yes, that is what I am telling you. I can't let him hurt you. I will not let anyone hurt you."

I want to scream at him, "YOU ARE HURTING ME! You can't keep me here I am not your prisoner!"

There is one thing I realize; I have to use his distorted state of mind to my advantage. I have to catch him off guard. Keeping him off guard will help my cause, or at least I think it will.

I quickly run through my head what he has done to many people, including myself.

I feel my blood boiling inside of me. He is standing close enough to touch, but not close enough for me to attack yet. I close my eyes for a second just to gain my composure, and when I open them, he is close enough to me now.

The moment is upon me. I must not wait any longer. The fight starts now. The fight, for my family, and me.

I take a quick glance at the ground. He has stepped inside of the chain. Perfect, just where I need him. A deep breath fills my lungs and I exhale quietly. I am about to try to take someone's life. It hurts *me to think of it even though this man is a sicko. He hurt Sam, and he wants to keep me a prisoner. I am the only one here to save me. I cringe as I lean in to kiss him. I am hoping he closes his eyes.*

Lola is chanting in my ear. "You can do this, you can do this." She has her Indian wardress on and her face still covered in war paint.

The bile tickles the back of my throat as I kiss Charlie. There is no turning back. I have to move forward with my plan this is for my

sister.   I scream CHARGE, in my
head.

As I am touching my lips to his,
he wraps his arms around me to
embrace me. I lean back against the
wall pinning his hands against the
wall, and my body. I bring the chain
up behind his back slowly, and as
quietly as I can.

I throw the chain around his
neck in one motion. I push my body
into the wall as hard as I can,
pinning his hands with my body
weight. I clamp down on his lip, and
try to bite a hole in it. Quickly I let

go of his lip as I give the chain a twist. I can taste blood. There is also blood all over his chin. I have such a tight grip on the chain that both my hands are numb.

He starts fighting trying to pull his hands out from behind me. God is holding me to this wall. There is no getting away. My body stands as heavy as a stone statue.

Thankfully, I feel his body going limp under my hands so I bring him to the ground. As I do, I land on top of him and with both hands; I tighten even more around his neck I can see his eyes are bulging and become blood shot as he struggles to breathe. He is pulling at my hair but I have my thighs draped across his biceps, squeezing them so hard they are cramping. He cannot get a good grip on my hair.

I smile down at Charlie. "Do you want to keep me your prisoner now?" Then without thought, I spit in his face. His face has turned several shades of purple. I know he is close to his last struggling breath.

I can feel his struggle is slowing down.

Suddenly I hear a voice that sounds as if it's coming from a tunnel screaming at me "Sarah! Sarah, you need to let him go! You need to stop, Sarah. It's Gideon. Let him go."

"No! He has to pay. This maniac got Sam hurt and wanted to keep me prisoner."

Chapter 18

∞

Gideon man handles me around the arms, and pulls me off Charlie. Charlie gasps for air. I can hear him choking.

"NO! You can't let him live! He has to die! I have to kill him." I squirm against Gideon, and kick at the floor trying to kick Charlie as he lies gasping for air on the floor.

Gideon throws me on the bed and jumps on top of me. He covers my head with both of his hands. I am sobbing uncontrollably now as I am screaming, "Let me kill him! God wants the world rid of these people. Let me kill him."

My body jolts into Gideon when I hear what sounds like gunfire. Then I hear a second sound and this time I know it is gunfire. I am crying uncontrollably still, and Gideon has his arms wrapped around me holding me very tight to his body. He is gently rocking me.

I do not know how long Gideon and I have been lying here when I hear him say, "Give us just a minute." Whom is Gideon talking to? And I realize we are not the only two in the room.

Tucker must have left the room at some point of my break down because he speaks from behind me. "Mr. Glass, you need to get Sarah out now. The clean-up crew will be here soon. I have the way out of the *house cleared so she will not see anything."*

Gideon rolls his body over the top of me. For a second I close my eyes and imagine that this is an erogenous moment. I grasp at his shirt not wanting him to get up. The look of fear on my face must have forced Gideon to lie down beside me again and hold me a little longer. I want this nightmare to be over, but I have to have him close a moment longer.

He hovers over me a while before saying, "Sarah, I need you to listen to me and I need you to follow me. I have to lead you out of this house. What is behind this door is not pretty. Charlie was not who you thought he was."

I want to ask some questions, but instead I bite my lip and nod my head to let him know I understand.

Gideon stands up in front of me and puts out his hand. I reach for it and he pulls me up on my feet. Without thinking, I look down at the floor, I guess to see what happened *to Charlie. There was a sheet over a figure on the floor. Somewhere inside of me was disappointment. I wanted to see him dead. I wanted to see the sicko gone. I know he is under there, I think I will be all right with that.*

I walk with Gideon out of the bedroom. He grips my hand tight as tells me to follow him and not look around too much. Why do people say that, because naturally what are you going to do, look around the room, right.

We are walking down the hallway of the house, when I remember Charlie living here as a child. My mind flies back to Sam and I playing hide and seek in his pasture as children. I remember seeing the house when he got mad at Sam and started walking toward it.

"Charlie grew up here, and I think this was his grandparents' house."

"Maybe." Gideon's mind is elsewhere, you can tell. I think he is worried about me right now.

This is an old shotgun house with a hall through the middle and rooms to either side. We walk past one of the rooms; I glance around what was once the living room. I try to pull away from Gideon's hand, but he looks over at me and shakes his head.

"I know you want to stop and look Sarah, but don't. Please just keep moving."

The walls of the once living room are covered with pictures like wallpaper. It took me a second to realize who some of the people were. Then the photographs came into focus and I could see the pictures were of me. Some of the pictures I saw were from years ago some of them are recent. There were also pictures that look to be slashed.

As we walk by the second room, I try to pull away from Gideon again. This time he does not just tighten his grip on my hand; he jerks me into his body under his armpit and gently wraps his arm around the top of my shoulder. I turn my head to try to look into the *room we are passing. Gideon places his forearm over my eyes gently and whispers, "You do not want to see what is in there." I am about to speak when, he catches me off guard by softly placing a kiss on my forehead. Suddenly I am at loss of words.*

The sun hits my face as we step out of the suffocating old house and onto the porch of Charlie Rhodes' family home. I close my eyes and take a deep cleansing breath. I realize one thing in this moment; I am free. God did as He always does; He kept me safe.

I wanted to find a church house so I could get down on my knees and pray. There is no church house in site, but this porch will do.

I drop to my knees, lock my hands together, close my eyes, and start to pray. I feel the porch sway a little and suddenly Gideon's hands are over mine. I open my eyes and look over at him. He has his head down, and his eyes are closed too.

We do not speak for a long moment. We are in silence together, praying for God only knows.

After the long moment of silence, I stand and start to walk off the porch. I grip at my chest realizing I want away from here, and now! I step off the porch into the yard and unexpected memories come flooding back in my mind. I summon up reminiscences of when Charlie lived here. For some reason I remember he lost his parents to a tragic car accident when he was younger. I cannot recall how old he was. I think soon after that is when he came to live here with his grandparents.

I can see all of us as kids again, running around the front yard and through the pastures.

Charlie's grandparents had a dairy farm here. There is not another house as far as you can see. We all ran for miles around this place as kids. I looked to the back of the house and I remembered there is a beautiful little creek back there. I almost wanted to run back there to *see if it is still there, but my desire to get out of here is stronger than anything else.*

These thoughts of Charlie, Sam, and I as kids almost bring tears to my eyes, but I refuse to let them. They do make my stomach feel queasy though. I grab at my stomach and try to squeeze the pain away.

I reach the SUV when I realize I want to know what Charlie has done. I wanted to ask Gideon if Charlie killed Lane. I never saw

Lane's body. I feel in my heart he did. I look out the window to see if I can see Gideon. He is standing in the middle of the yard with Tucker. They are deep in conversation. What could they be discussing?

Finally, they shake hands and Gideon starts lightly jogging to the SUV. He opens the door and climbs into the driver's seat. Gideon looks over at me and you can tell he wants to tell me to get in the back seat. Instead, he starts the car, puts it in drive, and peels out never saying a word.

We drive past all of the places that hold memories for me, deep memories. There is the old baseball field that I grew up playing softball on. We drive past the only grocery store in Hollow Springs, which was a Piggly Wiggly when I was a child. I can't remember off hand what it is now.

Gideon stops the SUV at the only stop light in town, and I have waited as long as I can. I want to know what happened. I need to know what happened. Furthermore,

why are the police not at Charlie's
house?

I have been looking at Gideon
for what seems to be a lifetime. I
can tell he knows I am staring at
him, but he is refusing to look at me.
He finally looks and I do not hold
back. I take a deep breath, and
spout out all the questions I have in
one breath.

"What the hell just happened
back there? Did Tucker kill Charlie?
Did Charlie kill Lane? Why are the
police not there at Charlie's
grandparents? Was Charlie the one

you and Tucker were looking at, as the man who hurt my sister? What else have you been hiding from me? You know I am not china, I can handle the truth."

I slam my body back against the seat and cross my arms. This is the best pouty moment I can muster up. Gideon doesn't say anything at first; instead, he turns the SUV away from town. This is weird. Why are we not going to the police station?

"Why are we not going to the police station? Chief Carson deserves to know about his son."

Gideon slams on the breaks, the car screams to a halt in the middle of the road. Gideon leans on the armrest. I get as close to the passenger side window as I can. For a second I think he may yell at me, but in a calm voice he explains, "Sarah, I thought you might like to see your sister. After Lane took you away from the hospital, Sam woke up."

I have no words. All I can do is smile. Gideon is grinning too.

"I am thankful that she did because she is the one who told us how to find you. Sam knew where Charlie would take you. Also Sarah, Chief Carson is at the hospital with your sister and he knows about his son Lane's involvement." Gideon looks out the window for a moment and adds, "I thought Chief Carson would like to hear about his son in person. Tucker will call the police to

Charlie's house once he is done there."

Someone drives by us as we sit, staring down the highway. They honk their horn and it wills us both back into reality. Gideon grabs the steering wheel and pushes the gas. The SUV roars back to life as it glides down the road and a smile comes across my face. I am on my way to see Sam! She is awake! When I see her this time I will be able to hug, her and she will hug me back. I think of Chief Carson and how his world is about to change as *he hears the news of his only son. My heart breaks for him. He has always been a good man. I do not know what happened to Lane.*

Chapter 19

∞

We arrive at the hospital and it seems like a lifetime before we find a place to park. Gideon finally pulls into a parking space. He puts the SUV in park and I reach over to open my door then he grabs my arm. When Gideon realizes he startled me, he quickly lets go. He puts his head down and rubs the back of his neck. I want to rub his neck for him when I see him.

"Sarah, I want you know Sam is still having a hard time. She is still not herself yet."

I look at him for a moment. I am not sure what to say. I decide not to say anything. I open the door and head to the entrance of the hospital. I am walking through the parking lot when I hear a car's tires squeal. I almost jump out of my skin. Then I remember there is no one alive to hurt me.

Gideon catches up to me. He is almost at a run. "Sarah, Sarah stop. I need you to stop."

"Gideon please, I need to get to Sam. I want to see my sister. What do you want? I understand she is not the same. I don't care. She is my sister."

Gideon does not speak, he just stares at me for a moment, and then gently he reaches for my arm. An inferno flares inside my body. I look around the parking lot. Then I think *to myself is this really happening here and now.*

Lola is jumping up and down in a nightie saying to me, "Really? Finally! Gideon is giving in! All my mind tricks have worked on him!" Of course, I giggle to myself, and at Lola.

Gideon pulls me into his body and raps his arms around me. His arms are so warm and cozy. For a moment, I forget what has been happening in my life. He is gently rocking me side to side, as we stand in front of the entryway of the hospital. Then it happens, what I have wanted to happen since the moment we met. Gideon pulls away from me and puts his hands up lightly he touching my face. I want to look at him, to see if this is really happening. Then softly he rubs his thumb across my cheek. I feel the rise of heat in my body as he touches me. My eyes close. I do not want to open them in fear this dream may end. I feel his delicate lips touch mine. A fire ignites inside of me and spreads along my body.

My blood burns for this man. I can feel my heart explode as Gideon gently tugs at my lip with his teeth. I am wondering why he is being so tentative. Then he wraps his arm around me and pulls me closer into his body. We are so close now we merge into each other. I melt with him as he pulls me in with confidence. Finally, he breaks the barrier of my lips.

My arms wrap around him as I stand on my tiptoes so I can pull him even closer into my body. I find myself running my hands through his hair. I want to grab it and pull, but I remember we are in public. Right on cue, I hear someone whistle. It catches me off guard so I let go of Gideon's hair and pull away from him. I look at him as I pull away and see his eyes are closed too.

"I have wanted to do that." He runs his hands through his hair as he adds, "And it was better than I thought it would be."

"Why Gideon, you are going to make a girl blush."

He grabs my hand, "Let me take you to see Sam. She is going to die when she sees us together like this."

I laugh, "You do not know how right you are Mr. Glass. She knows me, and she knows most of the time you are not that guy I would choose for myself." I drop my head down and stare at the ground blushing. "I think that's what makes me want you so much."

We are walking through the entrance of the hospital when

Gideon stops, "Why Ms. Wilds, are you stepping out of you comfort zone for me?"

I just give him a look that would drop anyone dead on the spot.

Again, we step out of the elevator on the ICU floor. I look around to find Chief Carson. He is nowhere to be found.

"Maybe he went to get coffee."

"Maybe he will be back when we come out." I am so excited I almost run through the waiting room. I reach the door that stands between Sam and me once more.

I tap the button on the intercom, and a voice says, "Yes, can I help you?"

"Yes ma'am, you can. I am here to see Samantha Wilds."

I do not get an answer I just hear a buzzer go off and the lock on the door clicks free. With excited force, I push the door open. Gideon stands behind me and I grab his hand and drag him in with me. We walk hand and hand around to Sam's room.

We stand in front of the curtain together. Sam is watching television.

"Hey, you."

Sam looks up and her face lights up. She pushes herself up in the bed, holds her hands out toward me, and smiles at me with tears in her swollen eyes.

I release Gideon's hand and walk over to Sam. I wrap my arms around her and squeeze. She winces in pain and I quickly let go and pull away from her.

Sam's voice is raspy and weak. "I'm alright Rosebud. Please hug me. I need to know you are safe."

I throw my arms gently around her this time. "CB, I'm better now. You had me worried."

All of the sudden Sam pushes me off her. I stand in front of her with a dumbfounded look on my face. She is frowning when she says, "Did I really see what I thought I saw?" She pauses, and then she points her finger at Gideon then back at me. "Were y'all holding hands when you came in here?"

Gideon steps in the room right behind me. He puts his hands on my shoulders. "You told me I would fall for Sarah, and Sam you were right. I have."

I stare at him in disbelief. I look back at Sam when I hear her squeal a weird low squeal come from her. She is smiling and laughing.

"Can you two let me in on the excitement, please?"

Gideon twists his arms around my body as he stands behind me. "For years Sam has said you and I would be perfect for each other." He kisses me on the side of my forehead as he finishes, "I always told Sam she was crazy. I would never fall for any sister of hers." Gideon's light smile turns to a serious one as he stares at me. Still standing behind me he adds, "Sam was right, I was wrong. We are perfect for each other and I have fallen for a sister of hers."

As Gideon leans into to kiss me, again I hear someone clear his or her throat. We all turn to see who it is. Sam's doctor steps into the room. He checks Sam over as we stay in the room with them. He asks her a few questions, and says she is holding her own with her breathing, and all vitals are good. Sam is now able to move into a room and out of ICU.

We all sigh a big sigh of relief then Doctor Carmichael looks at Gideon and I and says, "We may need to find you two a room of your own." He laughs, and I bow my head in embarrassment. "Hey, I am just kidding ya. I am going to get the paperwork going to move you." He looks at Sam, points the chart he has in his hand at her and adds, "I will see you in the morning. You better still be doing good."

Behind the Doctor comes the nurse. "OK guys, I need y'all to step out. I have to get Sam ready for the big move." Gideon and I scramble out of the room and for the door to the ICU waiting area. We get out to the waiting room and there sits Chief Carson. All the good that has happened is wiped out, and all the bad comes flooding back. I look back at Gideon and his smiling face turns somber. He sees Chief Carson about the same time I do.

Chief looks up from the paper, he sees me, and smiles.

"Sarah go wait over there," Gideon points with his eyes. "I need to talk with Chief Carson."

I grab his arm, "No. Don't go." He gently removes my hand and *doesn't reply, but instead walks over to Chief Carson.*

I turn to walk off and hear a person say in a low voice, "No, please don't tell me that." As I look up Chief Carson is heading toward the stairwell. He does not look back as he pushes through the door and out of sight.

Gideon turns and walks over to me. He sits down next to me in a chair he says, "Well that was different."

"That didn't take long."

"I know. All I said was Lane was at the house when Tucker and I found you. Then he said no do not tell me that and walked out. I didn't get a chance to him he was dead."

"Maybe that was for the best. This way he can find out on his own and we didn't tell him. He will find out soon enough anyway, at least right now he still thinks he is alive. I am glad you didn't have to tell him that."

"You know, I am glad I didn't have to do that either."

He pulls me into him with my face pressed into his chest, he encompasses me with his arms, and I lay my head on one of his biceps. I close my eyes and feel like I could sleep for days. It is the first time in a few days I have felt this way.

"Are you tired?"

"Yes."

Lola is lying on the couch. She has a t-shirt jersey on with a pair of white underwear. She has a sleep shield over her eyes, pink of course. She looks so peaceful. I am wishing

I were lying down looking so peaceful.

Right on cue, Gideon whispers in my ear, "You know, we need to let Sam get some rest. We can come back and check on her after you get some sleep."

Sounds so good as long as he is with me. I say in as sultry a voice as I can, "Will you be there with me? While I'm sleeping, of course?"

"Why Sarah, I would be happy to sleep with you; among other things."

I pull myself out from under his grasp and stand in front of him. Holding my hands out for him to grab, I ask, "Please take me. And sleep with me."

Gideon grabs both of my hands and I hoist him up out of the chair. We wrap our arms around each other and head once again to the elevator. Together this time we walk arm and arm.

A Piece of Book 2

By Stormy Raines

To be releases fall 2013

Suddenly, I am woken to then sharp sound of glass breaking. I lift my head from my pillow and look over to see the balcony door to my bedroom shattering everywhere. I roll out of bed away from the shattering balcony door and see bedroom door swing open. I quickly roll under my bed and lift the trap door.

"Lady, go! Go, Lady Ann!"

I hear gunfire as I close the all-metal trap door. Then I close my eyes and lock the door. As I am locking Grant out, I am praying to God to watch over him. The last think I need is to lose another bodyguard.

I wish all I could hear my hard breathing, but that's not the case. I hear a lot of yelling, and a lot of gunfire. I sit at the top of the stairs holding the lock on the trap door. I am in a hidden room tunneled out for easy escapes. However, I should be out there fighting, not hiding like a coward behind this door.

"Grant and Nila should not be alone," I say to myself as I lean my head against the wall.

"Lady Ann, you know there is no way you could put yourself in that situation. Grant would kill you if you were not killed in battle yourself. Stay put just as you have been told many times."

When I open my eyes, I notice the gunfire has ceased. No more voices. I quickly jump from my perch.

"Crap! If Grant does not find me at the safe point, I will still be killed!"

I begin my run down the stairs. Censored lights automatically come on as I run through the tunnel. I have always thought these lights were pretty cool because they are activated by retina scan only so not just anyone can turn the lights on. They automatically go off too after I pass them, good luck chasing me down here.

As I reach the end of the tunnel, I see Grant frantically screaming into his earpiece. It almost looks as if he is screaming at himself. Those earpieces crack me up sometimes.

"Nila! Have you found her? She is not here and I saw her go under

the bed as I entered the room!"

"Grant, here I am," I assure him as the lights come on at the end of the tunnel.